The Adventures of
Don Rogers

Volume 2

"Doing a Man's Job"

Douglas Murdoch

NEWMAN SPRINGS PUBLISHING
320 Broad Street
Red Bank, NJ 07701

First originally published by Newman Springs Publishing 2018

ISBN 978-1-64096-564-5 (Paperback)
ISBN 978-1-64096-565-2 (Digital)

Printed in the United States of America

Prologue

The year is 1946. As in volume 1, I am still fourteen years old and doing a man's job where everyone thinks I am eighteen. I drive Bob Kennedy's log truck, work at his sawmill, and live at the Salvation Army where Bob's daughter Pug works. Bob's wife Peg is a minister, and Sarah is Pug's older sister that is in her second year at the University in Eugene. My Uncle Elmer lives in a cabin that he built near Sutherlin. The rest of the people are important too and will be introduced later. Also, I hope that everyone reading this story likes coffee and cinnamon rolls.

Chapter 1

Sunday

Sunday morning and Pug was there with the coffee. I couldn't imagine starting out my day out any better. We sat down in the dining room, and she had some coffee with me. "Hope you can stay for a while. Dad is really depending on you."

"I know that. There's the mill, trade school, also you."

"Oh, Don!" She gave me a kiss.

Maybe we would have good news. The folks should have written by now. Elmer didn't have a phone though, so the only way I could do it was to drive over to Sutherlin in the morning and pick up my mail at the post office or go to Elmer's. Maybe if I got the letter, he would bring it to me before Saturday. But I guess, we could wait. In the meantime, we should leave it up to God and know it will be for the best.

"Would you like to eat breakfast out?" I asked to get my mind off worry.

"I would like that very much but let me see if Mom needs me first." Pug was back in a few minutes, and we walked to the café where Dot works. She was there and was surprised to see us.

We sat at a booth. I asked her if she had seen Bruce yet. "Hey, it's a little early, don't you think? I look forward to seeing him at 7:00 a.m., and that's what time it is right now. How about coffee? It's real fresh just the way you like it, Don."

"Yeah, that sounds good, and how about making us something special, Dot."

"Okay, and only because Pug is with you."

"Hi, Bruce!" Dot gushed. "I was wondering if you would make it in today. How about a kiss and I will bring you some coffee?"

"That's a good trade, Dot. We will be working the owl shift," Bruce said. "Looks like I will be getting up early as the crummy bus picks up at 2 a.m."

"We're going in early too. Hope to fill the pond by Wednesday!"

I had a real good breakfast and visit with Bruce and Dot. They might come by the Salvation Army for dinner and good music today.

After walking Pug home, I started with preventative maintenance on the log truck. Bob came out to see me, and I asked him when the oil filter was last changed. He let me know that it was changed last spring and the records are kept in the glove box.

"Here's the record. We've only gone 1,500 miles, so I guess it is good for another 1,500."

I showed him the oil stick, and it looks clean and right up there. I had a good look underneath and checked all the tires with a 2.5 pounds mallet.

"Bob, I cannot find anything wrong."

"That's good. Come over to the table and have some coffee." Pug was also there with some cinnamon rolls.

"Pug, these rolls are my favorite!"

"Mine too," remarked Bob. "Sure glad when you're here Don, never had all this pastry around 'til you showed up."

Well, it looks as though we'll try 3:00 a.m. and hope we don't get shut down if we can haul from four to ten that would work.

"I am looking forward to changing your mill to electric."

"Did I tell you that my instructor will help out when I have any questions so we can't go wrong. We'll be making so much lumber. We'll be liable to get short on logs."

"Don, I have enough timber tied up to last a long time, maybe a couple of years."

"I think I had better study for my quiz tomorrow. See you at the noon meal, Bob."

Back at my desk in the office, behind the counter, where Pug worked. She was in charge of all sales and bookwork. She never used the office, so I thought I could make good use of it. And that I did, several drawers were for personal things, like my hunting knife, compass, etc., and then underwear and socks in another. I used the other two for night school homework. After looking over the math, I knew I was ready for that class but still had more to do on the electric course. There were some work problems that I am figuring out.

Pug's calling for some help as it's close to serving dinner, which was between twelve and two on Sundays. I helped her set up for about twenty places and got the pitcher of milk out. The main meal was homemade beef stew, homegrown vegetables, and homemade dinner rolls. People were coming in. Peg was serving. I was pouring milk and coffee and bringing out the rolls with butter. Pug's mom came out and said a prayer and read a verse from Psalms.

About that time, Bruce and Dot showed up. "We heard you had the best food and music in town."

"You said that right and we'll prove it again." As Sarah strummed her guitar and Pug was on the piano. They started with "Amazing Grace," and I got the drums out and joined them.

There were more people to serve, so I took care of that. Peg blessed everyone with a prayer. Best stew I ever had, and the rolls were really good! Bob showed up for dinner as I guess he heard about the good stew.

We started up the music again, and the guests enjoyed it.

After "Rock of Ages," we played "Star Dust," "Georgia on My Mind," "Irish Eyes," and finished with "Amazing Grace."

Dot wanted to go to the movies and see "His Girl Friday."

"Anyone want to go with us?" Sarah said that she would like to see that movie too. "How about you, kids?" Pug said that she'd like to see it, and I said sure. Bob and Peg said they would stay and finish cleaning up. Everyone liked the movie, and we had a great time.

We went to the ice cream parlor, and everyone got cones. I had a single scoop as I didn't want to fill up. Dot and Bruce left us at the parlor. We bought a quart of ice cream to take home with us. Once we arrived home, I told everyone that I had some studying to do.

I was at my desk working on those electrical problems. Suddenly, I dozed off, and my head was on my book. Then Pug was there. "Don, are you okay?"

"Oh, sure, sometimes studying makes me sleepy."

"Maybe you need some dessert and it so happens I brought some from the house for us. Your favorite, chocolate cake with ice cream." I gave her a hug which brought on a *big* kiss. We managed to get to that cake and to the ice cream before it melted.

"Don, let's sit on the couch and listen to some music." We snuggled and talked for over an hour. Pug let me know that it was time for her to get back and that I needed to get back to my studies. "You can walk me back, Don." I liked that idea. I held Pug's hand, and off we went to her house. She kissed me and said she would see me at 2:50 a.m.

I studied for another hour and hit the sack early.

Chapter 2

Work Week

Before I knew it, the alarm was going off. I was at the truck by 2:50 a.m. Pug came with my nose bag (sack of food) and thermos of coffee. Had our start to the day, hug, kiss, and a cup of coffee. Bob showed up with the "carryall" (an old form of SUV). Bob got his sack and thermos and said that he would meet me at the site.

As he was taking off, I was climbing into the cab with my goodies. Pug bid me goodbye and told me to be careful. "Always," I said. I started up the truck and trailer at the cold deck, and Bob started loading my trailer. After a few minutes, my trailer was loaded, and I was putting the binders on.

Bob hollered, "Don't forget to retighten the load."

"Will do, see you soon."

It was mostly dark when I got to the mill. I could see the beginning of light in the east. I pulled into the log dump site and some lights came on. Tom came out to help me unload. "Boy, you are up early," I said.

"Well. I heard you coming and turned the lights on. Want some coffee?"

I looked in my bag and, sure enough, Pug had put a couple of cinnamon rolls. "Get your cup. I and have a cinnamon roll for you." Tom thought it was like a celebration. "I'll have to tell the girls that you like these rolls," I said.

I loaded up my truck with logs and was off to the landing area. As I pulled in, I noticed that they were doing a lot of yarding (removing trees from the forest). I got the trailer down and was loaded up in no time. This was my second load, and it was only 6:00 a.m. I was back at the mill.

Tom was on the pond. He came in and helped me unload. This pond would be filled in four to six more loads. I had a quick turn around and headed back to the landing. Bob shut down after getting the trailer ready to load. "Time for a break. Come on up, Greg! I finished off my roll with a cup of coffee."

I told the guys that Tom seemed to think another four to six loads would fill the pond. It looked like two loads on the deck. "How much in the draw? There is probably another three to four loads out there." Bob said that we should get as much as possible today as they could shut the woods down tomorrow. "Let's get this third load on the road."

We loaded and put the binder on within a half hour. Back to the mill and Tom was waiting for me. I got unloaded and was back on the road. I backed into the yard for another load at the cold deck (pile of logs). This is number four, and it's only 9:00 a.m. Bob loaded me up and put on the binders (chains). He decided that it was break time. I ate one of my sandwiches with a cup of coffee. I was ready to go when Bob told me that I should slow down some. We didn't need any mistakes.

I told Tom that there would be more loads today. Bob said to make sure that everything looks wet. Tom let me know that he would be right on that.

I drove back to the cold deck. It was loaded with logs. Bob let me know that once my truck was loaded up that he would be finishing up with yarding and would be done in about an hour or so. This would be the last load of the day. Bob reminded me to top off the truck with gas and that he would see me at home.

Back at the mill, Tom was on the pond, moving logs around with his pike. He was making more room for the logs. When he saw me pull up with the truck, he came in and gave me a hand rolling the logs off. He also helped me load up the trailer.

10

I started up old D-4 and pushed the brush pile further away from the burn site. Sure enough, there were some fire and hot coals underneath. Tom couldn't believe what he was seeing and let me know that I had saved them from a possible fire.

I got out my sandwich and poured some coffee into my cup. This was a good break. I watched Tom while he watered. I finished my meal up with the rest of my cinnamon roll.

I walked around the mill and checked out all the brush and trees that were on the perimeter. They looked okay, but I asked Tom if that water would reach that far. The humidity was dropping down and could reach the extreme danger point this morning. It is only 10:30 a.m., so you will have to keep pumping water on and off all day.

"By the way, Tom, how is the pump? What engine is running it?"

Tom said, "This is a 1937 Ford 60 HP flathead, and it's just above idle. These engines were only made in 1937 and 1938. They have a long stroke and are perfect for industrial work. These engines were put in their trucks and were a little short on HP so they went back to the larger flathead 85 HP."

"You seem to know your engines, Tom. I will talk to Bob about keeping a few around for back-up and leave this one on the pump. In an emergency situation, I would need that pump if the electricity went out."

"Yeah, that's good, Don. Well, let me see if this water can get out there further into the brush and trees. Have to go now, see you tomorrow."

Back home before noon and so I decided to wash the truck. I went to the office, and there was Pug doing the paperwork. We had a kiss and hug. I asked her about soap and a bucket with some rags so that I could wash the truck. She helped me round it all up, and I got the garden hose hooked up. I pulled the truck closer to the garden as a little water wouldn't hurt it.

It was a *big* truck and took extra effort to wash. I noticed that there was a "Kennedy Logging" logo on the doors, and I climbed up on the trailer and washed it too. When I was finished, I checked all the tires with the 2.5 pounds mallet plus levels for water, oil, and brake fluid. Everything was right up there. Just as I was finishing up with the levels, Bob rolled in with the carryall. "Don, can I have full service with a wash?"

"Yes, sir! Make sure your windows are up!"

I told Bob that I had checked the mill surroundings and had moved the pile further away again. There were coals and some fire in the sawdust. I asked Tom to hose everything down and, when I left, he was still in the process of watering.

"That's good, Don I won't worry about that now. It looks like four to five loads will do it. We have everything cold-decked.

Tomorrow, we would get it all to the mill. "After it gets light enough, Greg and I will make sure everything is out of the show. He and I can keep busy while you are moving the logs. We should still go in at 3:00 a.m. as they could shut us down at any time. I think that it will be okay with the loading as we won't be doing any yarding."

I started work on the carryall. It took me an hour to get it washed and check under the hood. It looked real good.

Decided it was time for some target practice, I set the target at fifteen feet which was near Bob's wood shed. I made about twenty throws with my hatchet, and all were within four inches of center. I sheathed the hatchet and did an 180-degree turn and then unsheathed and throwing only after my turn was complete.

Need to practice that and make it faster.

I looked up and saw that Pug and Bob were coming out to see me practice. Bob said, "You are good, Don. I don't think you can improve on this." I thought that I could speed it up some. Accuracy I have, but I need to get faster. I threw a few more and then sheathed my hatchet.

Pug thought that I should name my hatchet. This seemed like a good idea to me. She let me know two names that seemed good to her. They were "Protector" or "Savior." I wasn't too sure about those names and thought that I would think about it.

Bob let me know that we would be leaving at 3:00 a.m. again tomorrow. I let him know that the trucks were ready to go.

"I'm going to study and clean up for school. See you at dinner."

Boy, that shower felt good. I stretched out on the bed. I think I must have fallen asleep for half an hour or so. I woke up to Pug giving me some kisses.

"Thanks for waking me up Pug as I have some work to do." I gave her a hug and kiss. Off to the office I went and started my electrical terms and problems.

It seems that I am going to need some help on a couple of these problems. I guess that's where the instructor comes in. There are only two more weeks of these night school courses. In four more weeks, the trade school will begin.

Sure hope that I hear something from the folks this week. I wonder if Bob's going back. At one time, he was thinking of joining the coast guard. Pug just came in and let me know that it was time to start serving dinner and that she needed help.

Dinner tonight is corn bread, meatballs, potatoes with gravy, and carrots out of the garden. People were coming in, and we were serving after about twelve people showed up. Peg gave a short sermon. Peg and I sat down to eat the tasty meal. Pug said that they made up these meatballs last October from venison and beef mixed together with onions, celery, peppers and eggs.

We got up and served some more people. Peg said a prayer of thanks. We then played a few songs. It just rounded out the dinner and everyone clapped. Now that's what I think is a real help for those people, a good meal, prayer and music. I had another piece of corn bread and coffee, and I was set. We did a few more hymns and topped it off with "Sentimental Journey" and "Irish Eyes are Smiling".

I had to get ready for school, so I put my books together and told everyone I would be back in a couple of hours. Pug gave me a hug and a kiss before I left.

I got through both of my classes without a hitch. The teacher helped me with the electrical problem. He let me know that everyone has trouble with that one. If they don't get it, it will have an effect on the exam. I thanked Lou for his help.

I was back at the office by 9:30 p.m. I put my books and homework away and wondered where Pug was. There she was with two pieces of cake and getting some milk out of the frig in the dining room kitchen. "Here's our treat, Don." She wasn't kidding! A big kiss with a piece of chocolate cake! After dessert, we sat on the couch and listened to some music.

"It will be nice to sleep in until 4:30 a.m. again. Come on, I'll walk you home." We held hands to her door, and we had another kiss.

"See you at three-fifty," she said.

No sooner did I hit the sack, the alarm went off. I was at the truck at 3:50 a.m., and Pug showed up with the bag and thermos. She gave me a hug and a kiss. I poured out some coffee and climbed up into the truck with my coffee, lunch, and thermos. "Pug, I forgot to tell you that I've been giving Tom one of my rolls every morning. He sure likes it. One is enough for me anyway. I eat one-half at a time with my coffee."

I see Bob coming so I started up the truck and turned the lights one. "See you at the site, Bob." "Pug, could you check to see if the brake lights come on and then the turn signals? I forgot to check that out."

"Oh, Don, the brake lights are on, left turn, right turn. Wait a minute while I check your running lights." She jumped into the cab and said, "I guess you are ready to go now." I said good bye to Pug.

I made four loads before 1:00 p.m. This cleared the cold deck. One half of the last load did not fit into the pond, but they will roll in once they start cutting. We all decided to take a break as Bob and Greg showed up too.

Bob let us know that he had never seen that many logs in that pond. "Where have you been hiding the logs, Tom?"

"I have been doing a lot of piking. If I had fallen in, I would not have gotten wet that's for sure."

Bob said, "We really lucked out by getting all the wood in before they shut us down. As soon as it is daylight, I want this mill up and running."

"Greg, you can keep working, but it will be millwork. Don can check you out on the green chain, and you'll run the edger and cut off."

"Thanks," Greg nodded, "I'd like to keep working and then back to the woods when you need me."

"We have to keep the conveyers cleared off. The sawdust and the rest of it is going up that chute to the burn pile."

"Let's check each engine for oil and water and top them off with gas so we don't have to fool around in the morning."

"Tom, wet this area down even more than what you have been doing. You're doing good but we want it fire proof for morning."

"Okay, boss, you got it."

After checking out the engines, I drove the truck home and took a long hot shower. I stretched out on my bed and fell asleep. Pug came in to check on me. She was sitting on the edge of the bed. I could feel the pressure, and I woke up with one of her arms around me. "Pug, you sure know how to wake me. I laid down for a minute to stretch, and I must have fallen asleep. Hope I have enough time to do my school work." Pug let me know that there was an hour until dinner and that she would let me get to my studies if she could have a kiss. I told her one kiss was enough for now and that we could be together later when I got home.

It is really nice to have this desk to work on. I have been caught up for a month. I am always a little ahead of the assignments. With the electrical, it is hard to understand all the terms and theory. It will be better when I am doing the work and I can use the theory.

Chapter 3

Making Music

It is dinnertime now, and Peg read some verses and said a prayer. We served the people. Pug was warming up the piano. Peg started with singing "Rock of Ages" with Pug harmonizing. Sarah stood up with her guitar and joined in. It was something to hear. They went through several verses with me on the drums.

I made sure that everyone had enough rolls, milk, and coffee. Peg said another prayer and we went into some popular songs plus jazz and the blues. The guest were clapping with enthusiasm. Pug and I sat down to eat. Sarah and Peg did a couple of songs together with their beautiful voices. I had to leave and finish my homework. Half an hour later, I was on my way with a good-bye hug and kiss. "See you at 9:30 p.m."

Everything went good with my classes. I think I was getting better with the electrical. At least, I understood it now. There had been three people drop out as it was getting harder. If I understood the basics, then there's no problem.

Back at the office with the homework and putting everything away for the night. I met Pug at the dining hall where we would have our dessert at one of the tables. We decided to stay in the dining hall as there were no overnighters tonight.

"I made another cake today. Hope you are not getting tired of cake," said Pug.

"Heck no, I love cake especially your chocolate cake. Goes good with this milk. Hope I don't get fat." I replied. Pug let me know that she would tell me if I was getting fat around the waist. We gave each other a hug and then double checked to be sure we did not have any extra fat around our waists.

Pug said, "We will have to check every day."

"I left the drums out. Do you want to make some music?" I asked.

Pug said, "That would make some good starter lyrics. Let's write a song, Don."

"Yes, let's."

Lyrics: "We will make some music. We can make the music. We will make the song. Me and the music and the song, on and on."

"Sounds good with you singing it, Pug. Now can you write it down."

"Don, we have something we did together that means everything. Let's run through it a couple of times. I have the lyrics written down. Now we'll get the music to go with it. I can do that on the piano, and I know how to write the music too. Let's run it through a few times."

So we played and played until almost 11:00 p.m., and Sarah was there. She was worried about us. Sarah asked us if we knew what time it was.

We were so engrossed with the song we just wrote, and time got away. "Let's play it for her Don," said Pug.

"Okay, here goes with the same intro on the drums, and Pug will sing while accompanying herself on the piano."

Sarah was impressed and thought that we both had real talent. She also thought that her mom Peg and her could sing and accompany us on the guitar. We could then record it. Sarah thought that this could be a hit.

"Here, I was worried about you two!" Sarah said. "You might even be able to record an album! 'Don Rogers and the Kennedys.' Let's just keep this to ourselves now, and it will work out a lot better. I have a big day tomorrow. I guess we all do."

Pug told Sarah that we really loved each other. Sarah replied, "You two are just too much, and I love you both. I guess I could learn something from you, but you had better not get any more serious, physically speaking."

The girls accepted my offer to walk them home. "See you at 4:50 a.m. Good night, girls," I said. I gave Pug a kiss.

Sarah exclaimed, "Hey I saw that, and I feel jealous!" Sarah gave me a kiss too.

Chapter 4

The Mill

There we were at 4:50 a.m. at the carryall. Pug had two large nose bags and thermoses of coffee. We had time for a big kiss and hug. This got me started for the day! To top it off, I got some coffee from the new thermos.

Bob arrived, and we took off to pick up Greg. We arrived at the mill just when it was becoming daylight. Bob let me know that he had a good feeling and that today would be a good run. I would have to wait on running the headsaw as I would be busy with other jobs.

The first log came up the chute, and Bob had the first cut in a two by twelve. He held up six fingers. It was easy to run it through and came out with two by six's. Down at the cutoff saw trimmed off where they were sixteen-feet long. I helped Greg get started on the two-by-six pile. I pointed out where the two by eight, two by ten, and two by twelves went. Of course, I can't forget the two by four's. These piles of sticks go in every four high. I told Greg to holler if there is a question, and I will be right there to help out.

Here we go with another two by twelve, six fingers. The rest of the log was two by fours that were sixteen-feet long. Keeping an eye on Greg, I noticed that he would be okay. I showed him a certain way to stack where it is almost effortless. Greg picked this up quickly.

We shut down at nine for a break. We had a good stack of lumber already. I could see where the extra logs had rolled into the pond.

I got out my coffee and asked Tom if he had any made up. Turns out that Tom already had the coffee going.

Finished my coffee and walked over to check over the conveyer belts. I asked Bob how the humidity was. He replied, "I am not sure but will keep monitoring the radio. There is a new frequency now that gives out local weather which includes fire danger."

I reminded Tom now that he needed to water around the mill like yesterday. Tom went off to do just that.

We ran until about eleven-thirty and shut down for lunch break. Before eating, we had to get all the scrap wood and sawdust away from the conveyer belts. Once that was completed, the conveyer belt was turned on for a few minutes.

Got out a sandwich and it tasted the best! I had some more coffee and then started the old D-4 up. I showed Greg how to use it and how important it is to keep the pile moving away from the chute. If Bob had a burner like most mills, it would probably be safer and would not need to check it so often. We were not going to burn the pile until the lumber is off site.

Bob came by and let us know that we were doing really good work. I could see that Greg was getting the hang of it, but he would need some gloves and an apron to save his pants. Bob went to check the carryall for gloves and possibly an apron as well. "I told Greg that since you are always pulling to the right with the chain that he would wear his pants out in a hurry."

Before I knew it, it was after 2:00 p.m. It was time to shut down.

Bob was all grins and said, "We have been cutting 50 percent more lumber than we did before. You are right, Don. If we can keep this up, we will have it all cut before next Wednesday! It also looks like a break in the weather. Rain is expected Thursday, but there could be some lightning with it. Those lumber piles sure look good. Let's load up some of that scrap wood from the cutoff, Don. Okay, let's go."

Bob was telling Tom to keep the water on as much as possible until dark. Tom said that he would do it.

"You know what Bob said, it still looks as if the pond is full. You must have been hiding some of them. See you in the morning, Tom," I said.

Back home and I unloaded and stacked the wood. It sure felt good to take a shower once I had completed the work. I stretched out on my bed and as usual had a short rest. I went to the office to study as I had an hour before dinner. I was trying really hard to concentrate on my homework but kept thinking about Pug and my music. Shaking myself out of that line of thought, I returned to my homework. It was almost finished when Pug walked into the office.

"Don, stop what you are doing please. I missed you more than ever today. All I could do was keep thinking about our song."

"Me too, Pug. I believe that there will be more songs that we can come up with."

"Come close to me, oh, Don. We will have to be satisfied with what we have."

"Pug, that's another verse. Did you and Sarah tell your mom yet?"

"Oh, yes, and she's ready to work on it and go up to Eugene to record it. Sarah knows someone with a recording studio and knows we can do something with our song."

"In the meantime, we need to come up with a few more songs and try them out on our dinner guests," I said. Pug thought that this was a good idea. We planned to play our song tonight for dinner.

The milk was out and so were the rolls. Pug baked the dinner rolls and made homemade/homegrown vegetable soup. The soup was simmering on the stove, and it smelled good! I got the drum set out, and Pug got out her music sheet. I had her stay on the piano so that she could sort it out while I served the guests.

We only had six people so far, but it was still early. Some more people came in, and when everyone was seated, Peg read from the Psalms about music and being thankful. We went through several Gospels and then our new song. I guess it's a hit as everyone started clapping with a standing ovation. We then played "Sentimental Journey" and a few others.

More people came in, so I got up and served them. Peg said a verse from Psalms and a prayer. We continued with a couple more songs, "Amazing Grace" and "Onward Christian Soldiers," and ending with our new song and more cheers and lots of clapping.

Afterward, Sarah let me know that there were some changes to the song that we could make with the piano and the guitar. She would be working on the arrangement while I was at work. When she was finished, Sarah would show it to me and get my approval.

I walked over to the office to finish my homework. Just as I was getting ready to leave for school, Pug came in and kissed me good-bye. I almost did not make it to school in time.

Math seemed like it was getting easier. Lou, the electrical teacher, pulled a surprise test on us! Most of the class came out with 80 percent or more. Two of us made 100 percent. I was feeling really good about my test score, so when I got home, I bragged about my results. Most of our conversation though revolved around our new songs, which was more exciting to me. I listened to the song with all the changes. It did not seem all that different to me. I got out my drums and did the accompaniment. We had some overnight guests, so we had to stop at 10:00 p.m.

Pug didn't forget my dessert which was more of that good chocolate cake with milk. What a way to end the day! I liked how she never forgot our after-dinner treats. I hugged and kissed her, walked her home, and was in bed by 10:30 p.m.

I was at the carryall by 4:50 a.m. We had our goodbyes, and I got my coffee. I thanked Pug. Bob approached me and got his lunch. I picked up Greg, and we went to the mill.

The mill looked as if there had been a rainstorm. Tom was at the pond getting the next log ready. The mill started up, and we took a break at 8:30 a.m. It looked like it might be another good day with high output. This early break was my favorite as it meant some good cinnamon rolls! Tom approached with his own coffee. I almost forgot to give him a roll. It was great to see Tom chow down on the cinnamon roll!

Bob approached us and said, "It looks like rain. Sure hope we don't have any lightning. Let's get back to work, men."

We had another good day and it looked as though Tom did not need to get the hose out due to all the rain. We all looked at the pond and our lumber. Bob let us know that we had two days and all the lumber would be cut. I loaded up with more cut wood and pushed the pile further from the site. Bob and Greg were with me in the cab. After I dropped off Greg, Bob spoke about looking for a better price for our lumber.

The plan was to move the cut wood out on Tuesday. We discussed the possibilities of hauling it out ourselves so we could make more money. In order to do this, we would need a truck and a forklift. I thought that it would be better to hold off on this idea until we had electricity.

Bob thought my idea might be good. He would wait and see what the buyer thought of our last load. We might get a better price if he likes the quality of our wood. We were running two or better mostly, and no ones. Not many mills cannot say that!

"Don, can you wait for payday when I get paid?" asked Bob.

"Sure thing, Bob. I'll just take a draw."

"Don, I appreciate it. I have to pay Greg each Friday, or he will get another job. I would like to keep him on as it makes it better with another hand. He is great as an all around. Greg will be able to run the loader and set the chuckers when we are back in the woods. It makes it easier for me and makes it easier at the mill. When Elmer shows up on Saturday, we can have a business meeting and do some planning."

I unloaded the wood. It stacked really well as most of the pieces are eight by twelves. The shorter ones went into the crib. "I will see you later, Bob. I have to get ready for school and get smart. Hey, did I tell you that I scored one hundred on an electrical test last night?"

"I am really glad to hear that, Don. I hope that you don't get too big for your pants now," he laughed.

I took a shower and thought what a difference that makes! I laid out on the bed and thought maybe I have grown another inch. Pug came in and let me know that no one was here and how much she looked forward to seeing me. She lay down on the bed next to me. I gave her a kiss and got up real quick. I reminded her that that could happen later as we had plenty of time. I let her know that I had to study and get ready for class that night.

I went into the office and got my books out. I finished the math fairly quick. I will take algebra next time. I still had to work and concentrate on the electrical. I am putting a lot of effort into the electrical class as that will help me a lot when I get into trade school.

Pug came in, and I knew it was time for dinner. I helped her with the set-ups and getting things ready for the guests. She thought that there will be more than the usual guests as the word has gotten out about the music plus the good food. We set for fifteen again.

Tonight's meal was ham and split pea soup and lots of corn bread. It smelled so good!

Chapter 5

Louis and the Kennedys

I got the drum set out and ready to go. We stared to serve, and when we had served six to eight people, I told Pug to get on the piano and that I would continue serving. Sarah and Peg showed up, and Peg gave a short sermon and prayer.

At this time, the girls and their mom began to harmonize "Glory Be to God on High," "Amazing Grace," and "Rock of Ages." I joined in on the drums.

More people came in, and I served them and poured milk and coffee. I needed to bring out more corn bread, so I did that as well. Peg gave another prayer of thanks. The music started again with "Georgia on My Mind," and then I told everyone that we had a new one by Louis and the Kennedys.

We put everything we had in to the new song. Let me tell you that the people came alive with a large ovation and smiling faces. It sure looked like we have a winner. We finished off with "Sentimental Journey."

Pug and I sat down to eat and drink. People were asking who the new group was. Peg said that it was a new group and that there is no doubt that you will hear more from them.

I had to get my books and get to class. Pug gave me a kiss in front of everyone. She then asked me, "Where did you come up with the name for our group?"

"Well," I said, "my middle name is Louis, and you are the Kennedys. I think that sounds professional, don't you?" Everyone agreed.

Peg said "Don, you really amaze me."

I said, "Back at you all."

At school, we were told that finals were next Friday. We had a week to understand the information and come up with a passing grade for credit. It looked as though everyone would make it okay.

I told Lou that it looked like next Thursday would be the start of wiring the mill. He seemed really interested and wanted me to keep him updated on the progress and that he was available to help me if I ran into any problems.

When I got back home, everyone was still in the dining room. They wanted to know if we could go over the song again before we called it a night. I thought it was okay but let them know we had to stop at 10:30 p.m. as 4:00 a.m. comes around early. Turned out that there were no guests tonight, so we could make as much noise as we wanted.

I said, "This is a new hit by Louis and the Kennedys," and I added a drum roll. It sounded really good, and I didn't think it could have gotten any better. I said, "Let's get this recorded with the legal protection so no one can steal it."

Sarah said, "I know what you mean, Don. I will take care of it before we go to Eugene to record."

"How about setting up on Saturday or after next Friday as school will be over then," I replied. Sarah agreed that this was a good plan.

We went over the lyrics that we had come up with. Pug had written them down on paper, so now all we needed to do was add the music. We decided to go over the song a little more and then try it out on the guests tomorrow. I put the drums away and my homework.

I walked the girls home. They all gave me a hug, and Pug gave me a kiss. "See you at 4:50 a.m.," I said.

Chapter 6

Payday

It seemed like I had just lay down to sleep and it was time to get up again! I got to the meet up location, and there was Pug with two nose bags and thermoses of coffee. We had a *real* long hug and a couple of kisses. I liked starting the day like this. My coffee was really good! Bob appeared, and we both thanked Pug and said goodbye.

I told Bob that I was really looking forward to this day to see how much we cut and it's closer to tomorrow when I'll know for sure what's happening with me staying. I planned to stay but I just couldn't say for sure until I hear from the folks. Bob thought that the folks would go for it because then they would be rid of me.

"Bob, my instructor Lou, wants me to keep him informed on the Mill rework we are going to do. Do you have an in with the state so we can get the electrical permits?"

Bob let me know that he would take care of the permit today on the way home. We would need to shut down early, but since we were so far ahead of schedule, it would be okay.

We picked up Greg and had the mill running before 6:00 a.m. We had a break at 8:30 a.m., and Tom was pretty fast to come my way. I reached into my nose bag and got out a roll for him. I noticed that Bob was sharing his roll too. There was something about a cinnamon roll that really gave me a burst of energy. Of course, the coffee helped too. Break was over, and I put everything away and started up again.

Bob took longer to start up again as he was checking the teeth on the headsaw. Everything looked good, so it was back to work until 11:30 a.m. when we stopped for maintenance and lunch. I had a sandwich and a half with a couple of cups of coffee.

Greg needed help with cleaning up the chain saw and conveyer belts, so I assisted. We ran until Bob let us know it was time to shut down. It was 1:30 p.m., and it looked as though we got more board feet than yesterday. Greg showed us the results from yesterday and today as he marked each day's tally on a sheet of paper. Tom said that the ponds were holding about two days of logs. The rain helped us out as it was keeping everything wet. I got on the D-4 and moved the pile away from the chute. We cleaned and cleared all the scrap away from the mill. We were out of there by 2:00 p.m.

We dropped Greg off with his pay and told him we would see him on Monday. Bob and I went in search of the building department. They let us know where the state electrical permit office was located. As luck would have it, someone was in the office, so we got our permit. We were advised to keep the permit near the jobsite and to let them know a few days ahead of our turn on time. This would allow the inspector to be there to sign off on our electrical work before we could turn the power on.

As we left the office, Bob said that we were lucky because he had heard that it could take up to a week to get started.

"You know, Don, I forgot to give Tom some money. Let's take a quick run out to the mill," said Bob.

"Sure, I think we have plenty of time." I pulled out the rest of my sandwich and had some coffee with it.

Tom seemed happy to see us back. Bob gave him his pay. I overheard him tell Tom what a good job that he was doing and how he depended on him and the start time would be around 6:00 a.m. on Monday.

I told Bob that I would see him later and for sure tomorrow afternoon. I needed to hit the shower. Bob let me know he had a draw for twenty dollars. I let him know that was okay because our payday was when the buyer shows up.

I got in the shower and turned up the heat. I stretched out on my bed and went to sleep without thinking about it. I guess I wasn't getting enough sleep. I got about a half an hour and that really helped! I looked at the clock and it was 6:00 p.m. I was about an hour off.

I went to the dining room, and it looked as if things were slowing down. I helped myself to some milk, and Pug dished up some dinner for me. I told her I didn't want any, but she wouldn't hear of it. I couldn't eat very much, but I told her thanks and that I would have something later.

Walked over to the office to get my books and look over my homework, I thought I had it all done. I would find out when I got there. Pug saw me off, and I gave her a kiss and a hug.

Both classes went well except that I was taking more work home than usual. I think the teachers wanted to be sure that everyone passed.

Back at the office, I put my homework away and cleared off my desk. Pug showed up, and I told her how I felt as if I had lost an hour. "When I came home from work, I thought it was 4:30 p.m. and it was actually 5:30 p.m. I must have been in the shower when you showed up. I laid down for a minute and fell asleep for over a half an hour."

"Well, I knew that you came in late from work and didn't want to disturb you, as you have not been getting enough rest. I brought you some cake with a glass of milk. This cake is different. It is an upside down cake with lots of brown sugar, cinnamon, and butter along with pineapple," said Pug.

I did like the cake, and it was even better because Pug made it. We sat on the couch and listened to some music. The signal was strong and came from Eugene. Sarah knew the DJ that runs the 8:00 p.m. to 2:00 a.m. time slot. This meant that we might hear some of our songs sometime, sitting right here.

We sat there for a long time, talking about our future and just about everything else. I walked Pug home. It was almost midnight. "See you around 6:30 a.m. with some fresh coffee. Good night, Don."

Chapter 7

The Big News

I slept soundly for about six-and-a-half hours. I was still asleep when Pug showed up with the coffee. Good thing it was in a thermos as I wasn't ready for coffee yet. I think Pug knew I would still be asleep.

I came back from the restroom, and we sat in the dining room together. She poured our coffee. Pug rarely drinks coffee but when she does, she adds cream. I told Pug that I had to do the wash and get a shave and haircut. Bruce was meeting me for breakfast.

I think she wanted to go with me, but a guy had to do things on his own once in a while. I gave her some of my paper and had her write that down as it was some good lines for our song. I thought it would be nice if we had several songs to record at one time.

I told Pug when I got back, we could work together on the songs, and this evening, we could take a walk and get some ice cream. My big thing for today was word from the Folks by way of my Uncle Elmer. We had our hugs, and I was gone.

My wash was in the washer, and I went to the café. Bruce was already there. "Hey, Don, what's going on?" Bruce asked.

"Dot, that special would be fine for me. Tell me, Bruce, what's new with you this week?"

"Well, I got to work all week, partly on owl shift. The rain sure helped, and I haven't heard of any new fires. My company made me a head chocker, so I am running three crews now, and that's a sizeable raise."

"That's good news, Bruce. Don't spread that around or people will think you have money, and that's not good. Your friend Greg is still with us and seems to like the versatility of different work that's required of him. We're through in the woods for now, so he's helping us run the mill.

When we are out of woods, we will be wiring up for electricity. This electric project will be where my schooling comes in handy. I hope to see you at dinner on Sunday and bring Dot along. If you see Greg, tell him to stop over for good food and real good music."

I put my wash in the dryer and got caught up with the magazines, Dick Tracey and Superman. I left with my dry clean clothes.

I went to the barbershop. Four other guys and the barber were there. The barber said, "Hey, Don, we have been waiting for you. What is new with you?"

"Nothing is new with me other than putting in a good days work and hair growing out my ears and nose. That's about it. I guess I'll have the usual, hot towel and lower the ears one-half inch."

"Darn, Don, where do you get these," said the barber.

Everybody had a laugh. I told them that this was prime time for me and look forward to this every Saturday. There was a lot of talk, news and bull. I said goodbye to everyone and headed back home.

I put my clothes away and started my homework. I breezed through math and got going on the electrical. My real interest was in the industrial part of electrical and not the housing end of it. This reminded me that maybe Pug could check out that book for me again.

There was Pug. Seemed like she appears when I'm thinking about her. I told her about the book, and she thought we could walk to the library together today. I wanted to go now because I had to meet my uncle at 1:00 p.m., and we had plenty of time as it was only 10:00 a.m. She agreed and off we went.

I suggested to Pug that I would like her to carry a notepad with a pen or pencil at all times so that when we came up with a verse, we could write it down. It wouldn't matter what order it comes to us. We could sort it out later.

"Don, you are so smart," Pug grinned.

"Maybe so," I said. "You are the talented one. We make a real team!"

We set off for the library. It was located near the college. I found my book quickly. Pug was looking for hers in the business and song-writing section. She found one that cornered the ins and outs of recording. This would be a very informative book, and we could use it to help us. We were back home at noon, and I went back to my studies. I had yet to get some of it done.

Pug brought me a sandwich and a glass of milk plus an energy hug and kiss. I felt grateful as it was just what I needed! With that, I took off to meet Uncle Elmer, and there was his truck in the same place. I jumped in, rolled down the window, and rolled up a smoke. I was hoping Elmer had good news.

Before long, here came Elmer, strutting down the street looking clean from top to bottom. "Hey, Elmer! How's it going?" I said. "Do you have any good news with you?"

"Well, I didn't waste any time in opening that letter," Elmer said, "and well," he paused to remove his tobacco pouch and began to roll a smoke.

I couldn't take the suspense any longer and blurted out, "What did they say?"

"It's okay to stay for the trade school quarter and then make a decision on my staying later."

My heart raced. "Elmer, you had me going! I want to jump and shout!"

Elmer chuckled, then continued, "They said that Bob has to come back and finish school." I told Elmer that I thought Bob might go into the coast guard. We stayed a few minutes to talk about family stuff before we go over to the Kennedys.

I said that Bob was avoiding that gal that keeps chasing him. "He may not be ready to get married," Elmer said, "or he could go to Eugene next week and join up. That's his option, and I wouldn't want to talk anyone into doing either one."

"I would like to see Bob before he leaves. Tell him that I will make a trip up there to see him before he leaves. That would be better than him coming down here."

"Well, unless you got anything else, Don, let's go over to the Kennedys for our meeting."

The picnic table was waiting for us. The girls even had it covered with a plaid table cloth. Bob greeted us. Pug was setting out the coffee and a basket filled with cinnamon rolls. Before Pug left, I gave her and Bob the good news. She kissed me and ran into the house.

"After all the good news." Bob chuckled, "My news is second on the list, the main one just left for the house." Bob and Elmer had a good laugh. Bob continued, "Can't help but go after the rolls, what do you think, Elmer?"

"Boy, that's for sure!" Elmer said as he reached for a fresh cinnamon roll.

"Now that everyone's sweet tooth has been taken care of, we can get down to business." Bob began. "Can someone take notes as we might refer back to this meeting."

"Good idea," I said.

"Okay, Don, go see if anyone in the house can do that."

"Will do," I said. Bob told Elmer that Pug did all our book work and was majoring in business administration.

Here I came and Pug close behind with her pad and pencil. "Thanks, Pug," Bob began, "we discussed the date and time we hoped to get started on the electrical job. I told Elmer that we had the permit. It looked like Thursday and for sure on Friday to get started."

"What time of day do you get your mail, Elmer?" Bob continued.

"Oh, about 10 a.m., I guess."

"Okay, we could let you know by mail when we are starting, or Don and I could run up there and see you. It all depends on when I can get rid of my lumber."

Elmer said that we will no doubt need a welder and a cutter, gas would probably do. Not sure on the steel that we were using. The motors had to be mounted real secure, and they all came with rubber-mounted motor mounts. We went along on this planning for about an hour, and Bob adjourned the meeting.

Pug make a new file for our new mill. "Okay, Dad! This is exciting," she said, and she was right on that.

"Elmer, we'll either drop you a line or drive up to see you Wednesday or Thursday morning. Don has school in the evening, so we have to make it in the morning." It was 3:30 p.m. when Elmer left.

Chapter 8

Practice, Practice, Practice

Pug and I left for our walk. "Where would you like to go, Pug?"

"Is it too early for ice cream?"

"I think that's a good idea." We each had a double. I had a scoop of vanilla and chocolate. Pug had a strawberry and vanilla. We sat on the bench outside the parlor and ate our cones.

"Now that's a real treat, don't you think?"

"Where's your pad and pencil, Pug?"

"I have it right here and am writing as you talk. Don, you will have to keep a closer watch on me. Ha!"

When we were through, I looked at the coming attractions at the movies, and none seemed to interest us. We had more important things going on than a movie. Went back to the parlor and got a quart to go. We got back before dinner. Pug helped in the dining room and put the ice cream in the freezer. I helped out by setting up tables with a pitcher of milk and rolls.

No one has showed up yet, and it's almost 5:00 p.m. I got the drum set out and ready. Pug had three of our songs ready with the help of Peg and Sarah. I haven't had the time to practice but will do my best with the beat.

We served six people, and Peg read some Psalms with a prayer. We started off with some hymns, and some more people came in. I served them while Pug stayed on the piano. They sure sounded good, and then Pug played one of our new ones, and the guests were enjoying it a lot.

At the end of the song, I got up and said, "Some of the music you hear tonight has never been played before a live audience. It's a new group called 'Louis and the Kennedys,'" did a drum roll and the girls did a bow. We played another and there was a lot of clapping.

I did some more serving, and the dinner was very good. The best of home-grown vegetable soup with home baked rolls.

We played "Onward Christian Soldiers," "Sentimental Journey," and another of our new songs. The guests were sure happy, and they liked the music. But would people like it enough to buy the records? We had to work on these some more and give them the right names. I think there was enough notes that Pug has written down to do two to three more songs. It was 7:00 p.m. and had to close up the dining room and music. Pug mentioned that Saturday hardly anyone ever shows up, and the word is getting out that we have music.

None of the dinner guests were staying tonight, so it was for the food and music. Pug said after we clean up and put everything away, we could work on our songs. Sounds good, but first, I thought we should eat something. Pug said she forgot all about us eating.

We sat down and had a nice meal together. We both felt like we earned it and that always makes it better. Peg and Sarah said they would be back later to work on the songs.

I sat on the piano bench with Pug going over the sheet music that she had worked up. I thought the first one, "Music," is a go and the next one might be, we'll call this one No. 2, and we had a lot to do on the next two.

"Pug, I think we should polish up No. 2 and get it done. Then we will have two to record."

"Great idea, I know our song will be a hit!"

Here came Peg and Sarah with cake and ice cream for the four of us. "Wow!" I said, "chocolate cake and ice cream.

"Pug, did you make this cake? It's delicious. I can tell it's got a lot of TLC in it."

When we got through with the dessert, I suggested that we play No. 1 and then finish No. 2 before we start on the rest.

After an hour or so, we had 1 and 2 ready to go. So that's good, when we had a chance to go up to Eugene, we had two for sure.

"Sarah, thanks for lining this up," I said. "The evenings would be best, as it's after our dinner here and we could use Bob's carryall. Oh, that reminds me, does he have a drum set at the recording room and how about a piano?"

"I'll call him and get all the information. In fact," Sarah continued, "I'll go call him now, be back in a few minutes."

"Peg, can you please get an okay from Bob on this and then ask if we can use the carryall?"

"Okay, Don, will do. I think Bob will help us all he can but he doesn't want to be involved with this as he's really into our logging business."

Sarah came back. "It looks good," she said, "he works nights as the DJ for the radio station, and all the recording equipment is at his disposal. There is a set up drums and a piano. We can go up there tomorrow or next Friday at 9 p.m. as that is when he gets there. Probably, next Friday would be best for us as well get up early and work during the week."

"What do you think, Don?"

"Next Friday it is," I said. "Besides that, it won't interfere with anyone's work. We have to remember that Bob's company comes first as that's our bread and butter. Pug, write that down."

"Got it, Don."

Chapter 9

The Manager

We decided we needed a manager and of course a secretary and treasurer. "Nominations are now open for manager," I said. "Don, Don, Louis. Okay, it looks unanimous, and I would add that if I get too pushy, please tell me. Even though I am young, I have been making my own decisions for a long time, and I always wait for God to help me. I will be open to your help too.

"Nominations for secretary/treasurer. Pug, Pug, Pug. Congratulations, Miss Secretary!" I gave Pug a hug. Pug said we needed an assistant manager and nominated Sarah.

Everyone agreed. "Now, Miss Secretary, do you have that down in your minutes?"

"Yes, Mr. Manager." All had a good laugh and decided to have a work meeting after our evening meal and before I Don went to school. Not much time there but would get it in.

We called it a night, and I walked the girls home. Hugs at the door for everyone and Pug stayed for a couple more. "Pug, write that down."

"Okay", she said, "and write 'I love you' too."

Too late for my homework, so I hit the sack. And 6:30 a.m. was here before I knew it. Came back from the restroom and there was Pug sitting on my bed with a cup of coffee. I gladly accepted it. It took another coffee to wake me up some, and then I thanked her in many ways in the dining room. It was too dangerous to stay where we were.

The few people that stayed last night were already gone. I think they were just passing through. "That could have been me," I told Pug. Just passing through. "Pug, I'm glad that you were there to stop me with that wood-splitting job for your dad. I will never forget that day when we found each other."

"Where's your notepad? I am with you, Don," as she sat on my lap to get a little closer. She said that she needed the table to write on and sitting there put her closer.

Pug told me that she had a lot of lyrics in her note pad and that we could start on them today. "We could start on them now, or I could get my homework out of the way, and in about an hour, you could come back with more coffee and maybe a roll and how about another kiss?"

"See you in an hour, Don."

Got on my homework, finished the math in a few minutes, and right into electrical. I had my book from the library now and that helped put everything together so I could understand it. It was checked out for one month, and this time, I was going to extend that.

Here came Pug with a thermos of coffee, and it looked like cinnamon rolls. We sat down at a dining room table. The roll and coffee were the best ever! I told her that and also how sweet she was and a combination of love and sweetness all rolled into one, just like her cinnamon rolls.

We had to concentrate on our songs; we had plenty of material to work with. We had to write the music and match it with our lyrics. Now Pug was good at this; she was really talented.

"I think we can get two roughed out today, and the three of us can make the changes this coming week. Can Peg play a guitar? We should have a base along with Sarah's."

"Oh, sure, she plays all instruments," Pug nodded.

"That's what we need, so let's try to get one tomorrow, maybe at the hawk shop, or do we have one here?"

"We don't, but Mom, Sarah, and I will pick one up along with new strings."

"You are the treasurer, so here's twenty dollars to put in the pot. I could put more in but won't get paid until we sell the lumber, maybe Thursday."

"Don, I think you are right on base. It would make us sound more professional."

"You know what, Pug, I should try and learn the guitar or piano. There should be a portable piano like a small organ, all electric."

"Well," Pug said, "there are electric guitars, the Rickenbacker and the Fender, but they all need amplifiers with speakers. The best thing for us is the acoustic guitar. Don, you are real good on the drums. You could learn to take over on the guitar or piano when needed, but that's down the line a bit. I'll keep helping you with the piano for now, okay?"

"Sounds okay. Thanks Pug."

Pug said she had better help out with dinner preparations. "I will be back to set up around eleven-thirty. I think there will be more guests than usual. This is a good time for homework, have to work out some of these electrical problems."

Before I knew it, Pug was here in the office and asked me if I would help her set up for the guests. We decided to set up for twenty-four, as word was getting out about our good food and music. We had better play more religious songs than we had been as we didn't want any trouble with the main office.

We got all the set-ups out, and I found another pitcher for milk. We were to have spaghetti and meatballs with garlic toast. "Sure smells good," I said, "make sure there is enough left for us!"

"Don't worry. There's enough here for fifty people!" Pug said.

Chapter 10

Bigger Crowds

Here they came, and we started to serve. When there was about twelve people seated, Peg read some scripture and said the Lord's Prayer. This was followed by some gospel music while I was serving more guests and pouring more milk and coffee.

Bruce and Dot showed up with Greg and some other gal. We served them, and I gave a welcome to everyone. Peg read some more from Psalms with a prayer of thanks and we started with "Glory Be to God on High," and "Onward Christian Soldiers."

I got up and told everyone about the two new songs from Louis and the Kennedys. There was some clapping, and we took off with me on the drums. Boy, they were a hit! Then after the applause, we went into "Amazing Grace" and "Sentimental Journey Home."

We all sat down to eat and ended up across from Bruce and Dot. Dot couldn't get over the songs we wrote. "You kids are really talented," she gushed. Of course, that is meant for Peg and Sarah too. Sarah thanked everyone for coming to dinner, and they also thanked us again for the great meal and good music.

"I guess it's like going to dinner theater up in Eugene," said Bruce. Just then, Bob came in and asked if there was any spaghetti left. Peg said there is enough for a dozen hungry loggers! I had another helping with that garlic toast. Filled up my milk cup and made sure all the guests were taken care of.

Some of the guests asked if there was any more music. "Will try and do that," I said, "in a few minutes." I finished up my plate and poured everyone coffee. Peg read some scripture and said a prayer. We played "Amazing Grace."

I then got up and introduced the band, "We are Louis and the Kennedys with a couple of new songs that will be hits, and you heard them here first." I did a drum roll, and we got underway and played music, music, music. I was afraid they wouldn't stop clapping, so we went into our next one, and it sounded as good if not better than the first.

After it calmed down some, we played "Irish Eyes are Smiling" and thanked everyone for coming and closed the evening with an audible prayer.

Bob could hardly believe it. "You are all amazing and to think I'm the dad to that group and Don, and you all are something special." After that, we had another helping. It was a good visit and sure fun being around these friends, but I was trying not to appear as excited as I was inside. Some people asked if it was all right to come back again.

Pug said everyone was welcome any time and to use the envelopes on the tables for contributions. But our main contribution was all of God's children being full with the Spirit and not leaving here hungry. "Amen to that," I said.

"Where are you all going?" Sarah asked.

"We thought we might walk downtown to the ice cream parlor."

"If you'd wait a few minutes, we'd like to join you."

"You, kids, go ahead. Dad and I will stay here and put things away. Maybe you could bring us back some ice cream."

We had a nice walk. It wasn't too hot out as that rain the other day cooled things off pretty good. It was in the 70's, and no more talk about the woods shutting down. We had a good walk to the parlor. A walk is always good when you're with friends.

Pug and I had a single scoop. I think Sarah had a double. Bruce wanted to pay so I let him. We all hung around the bench outside and ate our cones. "What flavor shall we get to take back?" Pug said. That didn't matter as the folks liked all flavors.

"How about a quart of vanilla and one strawberry?" Sarah said. Everyone agreed.

We had a lot to do and plan and headed home. Bruce said, "See you later, Louis and the Kennedys." We got back home with the ice cream and started working on our songs. After an hour, Pug and Sarah went to their house and said that they would be back in a few minutes. This would be a good chance to practice on the drums. I was really getting with it and felt like I was in the zone when Pug showed up.

"Don! Are you with us?"

"Oh, sure, I am here now, especially since you are here and with dessert too."

"Yes, we're here," as she sat on my lap and gave me a large kiss.

"Let's put the other dessert in the freezer and take a walk."

"Hey, that's fine with me. I have to check in with Mom first."

We decided a walk to the park would be nice. For once, no one was at the horseshoe pit. So we thought throwing some shoes would be in order. Hadn't played for a while and it felt good. Pug was staying up with me, so I laid down a couple ringers. "How did you do that? Show off!" Pug made a ringer and the games was close.

"How about playing the winner?" a familiar voice boomed out. It was Bruce.

"Okay," I said, "for twenty-five cents."

"Hey, that's not enough." I said that I couldn't afford to lose more than that and we all had a good laugh. Dot was with him and said that I thought you said that you, kids, had lots to do at home. We did but had to take a break.

"Well, Don, it looks like you won. Just barely though twenty to eighteen."

"Pug, you're getting better and hard to beat."

Bruce and I started even. Each had double ringers, and our next throw, he put on two ringers and the last one backward. So guess what? I knocked that off with a ringer and put another on top. This put me ahead. I think he did that on purpose. I really concentrated and put on two more ringers. I was ahead and I could beat him if

I didn't miss one. I didn't make it as I missed two more, and Bruce won.

"Good game," I said and "I know you put that second horse-shoe on backward as planned." Bruce said that we both have back up work any time we need it.

"That's for sure, Bruce. We are a team, a winning team." Pug and Dot agreed that we were the best and decided to keep us close. With that, we said goodbye for now as we really had to get back and work on our music.

When we got there, the first thing we did was get the dessert out of the freezer: berries, ice cream, and cake. We let it sit a few minutes while we had some hugs. After the dessert, we went to work on our music. Pug had changed some of the arrangement, and I think it was sounding better.

Pug went to the house to tell them that we were back so they wouldn't worry. It was getting late as it was already 9:00 p.m. We had an early start tomorrow.

I went to the house and said good night to Pug and told her that we would see each other at 4:50 a.m. I put the drum set away and was in bed by nine-thirty.

Chapter 11

The Fender

U p at 4:30 a.m. and ready for a big day. We had our usual send off at ten to five, and it was great, even the coffee.

We're at the mill and had her up and running before 6 a.m. Tom had the logs lined up, and it looked like there was more in the pond than on Friday. We had a big day and it looks like we can finish off all the logs by tomorrow or Wednesday for sure.

Back home, I had my shower. Didn't fall asleep this time and was up when Pug showed up. We had a big hug, some kisses, and talked about our day. Sarah and she had found a real neat guitar, old but in excellent shape. A Fender and she knows her guitars. They wanted sixty dollars for it, and she ended up paying forty-five dollars with a set of strings and some picks. I couldn't wait to see it!

Here came Sarah now, and it even had a case. Not a pretty case but very used-looking one which I thought was good.

Sarah took the guitar out of the case and handed it to me and asked, "How does it feel?" It felt like it belonged and fit perfectly. "Don, you can start getting familiar with it by replacing the strings. Here is the pamphlet of guitar basics which you will need to learn." As I was holding it, I did a couple of chords, and it sounded really good. It fit me so good, I had to learn how to play it.

We got ready for the dinner guest, and I put out the set-ups along with a pitcher of milk. Got the drum set out, and it looked to me like we were ready. We had about twelve people. After Peg's readings and prayers, we began to play some songs. Mostly gospel and did our two (hope to be) hits. There was a lot of clapping. We went with a couple more including "Sentimental Journey."

After that, I had to eat as a working guy gets hungry. Got off to school. I went over both subjects because finals were coming up on Thursday. Back home at 9:30 p.m.

There was no one there except for the new guitar. I looked over the instruction book, and on the first pages were instructions on changing the strings and how to tune it. Before I remove the old strings, I thought I should practice tuning on them. The piano helps me with the tuning and the rest of it by ear. After ten minutes or so, I got it tuned really well, I thought.

The guitar book showed me the chords, frets, and where to hold my hands all the basic stuff. I turned a couple more pages and there was the first basic song, "Twinkle, Twinkle, Little Star." Within a few minutes, I had it and it sounded okay.

Pug showed up just as I was putting away the new strings. I wanted her to think I changed the strings so I could test her to see if she could tell the difference.

"Hi Pug, get a load of this, Twinkle, Twinkle…"

"Don, how did you do that and those new strings make it sound a lot better. Bring one of our new songs out and help me keep up with you on the piano. Here is the music with the chords called out. Okay, let's go."

We ran through "Music, Music" several times, and then we sang the lyrics. "Don, we really have the song thing going on. Write that down."

"Okay, 'We Have Something Going On.'"

"Got it and, by the way, brought you some dessert, white cake, berries, and ice cream." Wow! Was that ever good. When I was finished, she had an encore. I told her that it's time to be walked home.

"If you say so, Don." I told her I looked forward to ten to five and had a good night kiss. I walked back to the dining room where I put everything away. Not only do I have the responsibilities for the drums but now that beautiful guitar too. I put her in the case and made a place on my desk. I hit the sack, and before I knew it, it was

4:30 a.m. I just made it for my ten to five date. Pug was there with my thermos and nose bag. "Pug," I said, "you make it all worthwhile, and I look forward to each new day."

"Oh, Don," and she gave me a big hug and kiss.

I filled up my coffee cup. Bob pulled up, so I jumped in and off we went. We picked up Greg and arrived at the mill before 6:00 a.m. As we pulled up, I noticed Tom was in the pond getting the logs lined up. We started to work and didn't stop for a break until eight-thirty.

Tom came to our break table. I shared one of my rolls with him. It was a great break especially with the best rolls and coffee in the county!

Greg and I cleared off the belt and ran the excess sawdust and scrap out of the chute. Bob checked the saw teeth, and everything looked good.

"Let's fire it up!" Bob hollered.

We stopped at eleven-thirty for lunch. Tom said that we were down to six more logs. Bob said we had two more hours to run and that he had talked to the buyer last night. The buyer would be out today to look it over and scale it.

After lunch, we checked out all the belts and cleared the chutes.

"Let's fire it up!" Bob shouted.

By 2:00 p.m., we ran out of logs. We trimmed the last board and helped Greg finish stacking lumber. Then ran all the scrap and saw dust out the chute.

Bob came out to the lumber with his clipboard. He counted the piles, and Greg helped him measure each pile. This will give us a pretty accurate scale of what we had. It was close to 30 percent more than over the last sale. I am thinking that it will be a pretty good pay day this Friday.

We all took a break, and Bob gave us the plan for the rest of the week. "We'll start to work in the mill at 0700. Tom was to soak down the area real good this afternoon. This reminded me to push the sawdust pile away from the mill. I loaded up the carryall with scrap wood from the cutoff saw."

When the buyer arrived, Greg and I sat down at the table and took a coffee break. The buyer was looking over the lumber, and Bob had his figures and was waiting to see if they were close. Turned out that the buyer's figures were higher than Bob's. Bob did not let him know that. Also, Bob held out for a better price than last time.

The buyer let Bob know that the truck driver would have the check for him. He gave Bob the amount of the check.

We were on our way home before 3:00 p.m. We took Greg home. Bob told him that we would pick him up at 6:30 a.m.

I unloaded and stacked the wood. Bob said that it was nice to see all that wood. He also let me know that he had never been so caught up with the work at the mill and at home. He was glad that I was there. I thanked Bob and told him that I like to do my share.

I walked to the office and no one was there. So I went out back, and I threw my hatchet several times. I was right on the mark.

My daily shower felt really good. I laid down on my bed to stretch. I thought, *Now this is the way to end a day's work.* I looked up and saw Pug which made it even better.

I told Pug that I didn't have homework, and we would have more time to study our music together. I got the guitar out, and Pug went through some chords with me. "Let's practice one piece until you get it down good enough to play it tonight that will really surprise Sarah."

Chapter 12

Sounding Good

"Which song do you have more feeling for and can hear the notes in your head?" Pug asked me.

"That's easy. It is our new one, 'Music, Music.'"

"Okay, Don, let's hit it. Here's your sheet music on the piano which you shouldn't need after a couple of times through it. I think you should try the vocal also." I breezed right through it, but I wasn't sure how it sounded.

Pug thought it sounded good. We tried the song again with her singing with me. I thought that was better. We practiced three more times, and we made changes as we went along. Just like we knew what each other was thinking. Like we had our moves down.

There were only three different chords on that song. I had those down good enough so that I didn't need the sheet music. I brought out the drums, and I would alternate between them and the guitar on the other songs.

It was time to get ready for our guests. I put out twelve set-ups and a pitcher of milk. We had corn bread that Pug had baked along with ham and scalloped potatoes.

People came in, and we started serving. Peg was there with some good verse and a prayer. Sarah was also there. We went through a few songs, and some more people showed up. I served them and got back on the drums.

We did "Christian Soldiers," and then I thanked everyone for being here. I told them about our new song and how we wanted to see how they liked it.

I picked up my guitar, and Pug started out just like we had practiced. Some people clapped before we were finished. It looked good, and we were waiting to hear from Sarah.

Sarah lit into me with, "Dog gone, it sounded so good on the base. Don, you are just too much. I can't believe it."

"Well, Pug has been helping me." We finished off with "Sentimental Journey" and "Irish Eyes Are Smiling." We sat down and ate dinner. It sure was good!

While Sarah was with us, we tried out the other new song. There were only three chords in it also. We went through it several times, and it looked like I got it. I told the girls that I couldn't have done this without them. I really felt like part of the group.

Pug wanted to go over the two again and make changes where it may complement the song. After a couple times, I had to make my classes. I asked the girls to take care of the new base. I loved it! Kiss and hugs all around and I was gone.

At each class, it was more review for the exams on Thursday. I was back home by 9:30 p.m. They were still working on the other two songs. I put my books away and got a hold of that base. I did some chords and tried to play along with the girls.

Sarah said that we might be ready with all four by Friday's recording. If the last two weren't 10 percent, then it would be better to wait until they were as good as or better than one and two.

"Don, work on number three and four tomorrow. We will see how it all sounds on Thursday. We can try it out on our guests. Oh, yeah, I almost forgot," Sarah grinned, "we have a special treat for our manager!" Pug brought her famous chocolate cake and a cup of milk.

"Thanks," I said, "is this from Pug's bakery?"

"Yes, with TLC."

"Where's yours?" I said to Sarah.

"I already had mine, but Pug might want to help you with that one. I am going to leave you two with that cake." We walked Sarah home as its pretty dark out there now. At the door, we both got a hug from Sarah.

Chapter 13

The DJ

We sat on the sofa and tuned the radio to the DJ from Eugene that was Sarah's friend. "The cake is really good, have some Pug."

"Okay, just a small one as I'm always sampling all my baking, and you might not love me if I get too fat."

"A little fat would be okay," I teased, "but how would I know if you were getting heavy?"

"You could check my spare tire every day and lift me off my feet. If I feel good to you then you have to keep loving me," Pug giggled.

"Now that sounds fair enough for me. I guess we could start checking you out tonight. Okay, let's see, now I don't feel any spare tire."

"Here, let me help you. It's around my waist."

"Well, it looks like you are thin enough."

"You, silly thing, you never checked it enough."

"Well, maybe next time, I'll do a better job. Here let me lift you up. There, I did that right."

"You just need more practice." We had a good laugh and then tried to listen to the radio.

"Oh, by the way, did your dad tell you we're leaving at 6:30 a.m.?"

"Yes, he said about 6:25, so I'll see you at 6:15."

We got back to the radio. There was a spot where he gave info on the station and a couple of ads. He just said the station was in Eugene. He was telling his listeners to be sure and stay tuned this Friday night, and this weekend he would have some surprises for them.

I walked Pug home and kissed her good night. "See you at 6:15." I got back and made sure everything was put away. I hit the sack.

I was out at the carryall at 6:15 a.m. I had some hugs and kisses to start the day with that necessary cup of coffee!

I talked Bob into keeping those engines. For now, they could be stored at the side of the mill out of our way. Once the electric motors and panels were installed, we could bolt down the engines on the platform where the electric meters were stored.

By 9:30 a.m., we had a good start on removing the engines, so Bob shouted, "Break time!"

I got my coffee and opened up my nose bag. There was the cinnamon roll that I had been thinking of all morning. Just then, Tom came over to sit next to me. I said, "Hey, look what's got your name on it," as I handed him a roll.

The lumber truck pulled in and parked. The driver looked over the piles of lumber and let us know that it may take three trips. He handed the envelope to Bob. We helped him get the forklift off the trailer. The trailer was loaded up, and the truck was on its way within the hour.

After finishing my coffee, I went back to work. We took a lunch break at eleven-thirty. The truck pulled in for its second load. We had the truck loaded by noon. The driver let us know that he would get the rest in the next load.

At two-thirty, the truck arrived for its third and final load. After the driver was finished loading up the truck and trailer, I thought it looked overloaded. The driver said he was legal weight, and that he had it all on, including his forklift.

Bob said, "Let's call it a day. Tom, give it a good soaking again. See you at 7 a.m."

It seemed like Bob was in a hurry to get home. We dropped off Greg and went to the bank with the check. "It is a big relief to deposit that check," he said. "Now I can pay some bills and hope it gets us through until the next sale."

"Bob, it looks as though we can get the mill up and running in a week. If it looks like we can't, we can go back after dinner and work another four to six hours. I can rig up some lighting, and Elmer will be there to help. When we get close to finishing, you could take Greg, set up for another show, and maybe fill up the cold deck."

"Hey, Don, that's a good idea. We may save some time that way."

"Later, Bob, I am hitting the shower and getting ready for school."

I took a shower and laid out on my bed to stretch. Then I hopped up, taking out my guitar and playing some chords and singing along. I sure liked the feel of this guitar. It just seemed to fit me.

Pug came in and gave me a kiss and said how good I sounded. She sat at the piano, and we went over songs three and four.

"It looks as though we will be ready to record all four songs," Pug began. "Maybe the best thing to do is only release one each week rather than play them all at once."

"Sounds good to me," I said. "I will talk this over with Sarah and see what she thinks. In the meantime, we can play three and four for our guests tonight."

Chapter 14

The Dinner Show

It was time to get ready for our guests and get the instruments ready. The Fender sure looked good leaning against the drum set. We were ready, and some people started to show up. Pug and I had served about eight guests, then Peg read some scripture and said a prayer of thanks. Sarah and I joined in and read a few gospels.

More people started coming into the dining room, so I served them while Pug and Sarah sang "Onward Christian Soldiers," with me on the drums.

Peg said another prayer with some more scriptures, and then I got my guitar on and introduced our band as "Louis and the Kennedys." I welcomed the guests that were there for dinner. I also told them that we had some new songs to try out on them. Pug started out on the piano and Sarah followed her on our guitars. We finished song three and had a lot of clapping. When it quieted down, we went into song four.

I switched back and forth from guitar to drums when it was necessary. This song really sounded like a hit. When we were done playing, there was loud clapping and yelling for more. I thanked them and there was more clapping. We went into "Sentimental Journey" with "Irish Eyes are Smiling" as the ending.

Guess who was there all the time? It was Bob, and he said that he thought we really had something there and could hardly believe it. "Don, where did you learn to play the guitar?"

"Well, from Pug and Sarah, and the rest was in me wanting to get out."

I ran out of time and had to get to my classes. "When you get back, we will have a late dinner for you," Pug said as she hugged me.

"Thanks, Pug."

On the way out, I grabbed a dinner roll with butter on it. At school, both classes were studying for our exams tomorrow. I knew that I might get 100 percent on both subjects. When I got back home, Pug had dinner laid out for me in the dining room. No guests stayed over. They come for the "dinner show." I filled up fast and told Pug that I couldn't have any dessert tonight as I was too full, and besides, she was my dessert!

Well, that did it, and besides I wanted to turn our DJ on. Good music and he might mention Friday night again. "Isn't that great that your dad liked us so much, maybe he'll want to go with us to record on Friday."

"There's our DJ now. He sure tries to sell a lot of stuff."

"That's what you call advertising and that pays for the program," said Pug. We listened to him and some good music for an hour.

I told her that it's time to hit the sack. "I will walk you home." At the door, we had a good night kiss, and I told her, 6:15 a.m.

Chapter 15

A Good Day

I got up at 5:30 a.m. and had plenty of time to be at the carryall before 6:15. Pug was carrying two bags and two thermoses. She gave me my nose bag, coffee, and a kiss. Bob showed up, and I poured myself some of the good coffee. We said our goodbyes, and we drove off to pick up Greg.

It was a good day at the mill. I removed all the engines and started installation of the electric motors. Boy, that was fun, and before I knew it, the workday was done.

I had a hot shower and stretched out on my bed. I must have gotten in a short nap. I opened my eyes, and Pug was sitting on the edge of my bed waiting for me to wake up.

She asked me to go over the songs with her. I told her that I would, but I would rather practice after school tonight. "I'm rather nervous about the exams and need some time to think about them. When the exams are over, I can give it my all."

"Okay, can't wait Don."

I went to the office and got my books out to study. I heard Pug on the piano and Sarah on the guitar. Eventually, I had to join them as I couldn't concentrate on my homework. I got the drums and the Fender out. I joined in with the girls, and we made some good music. We decided that we would play all four songs tonight, with me alternating between the drums and the base.

It was close to 5:00 p.m., and we got ready for our guests. There was spaghetti and garlic toast for dinner. It smelled really good! We put out twelve set-ups and a pitcher of milk. Also, we had a tossed salad that the girls put together.

When there were eight guests served, Peg read some from Psalms with a prayer. We played some gospel and more people showed up. I did the serving while the girls did a couple more songs. Peg said a prayer of thanks to the Lord.

After that, I welcomed everyone and introduced the group as "Louis and the Kennedys." I let the guests know that we had some new songs that we would like to play for them.

We did all four songs. At the end of each song, we had an enormous amount of clapping. We stopped after the fourth song and thanked them. We had a lot of requests for more, so we did an encore of song number four. Sarah said that she thought this was awesome! We all bowed and thanked the audience. I couldn't remember afterward what I had said. I think it was, "We thank you. We thank you very much!"

We had our dinner, and it was very good. I said goodbye to everyone, and they wished me the best on my exams.

I was the first to finish with the math exam and had to wait until everyone else finished. He called each one of us up to his desk. The teacher told me that I got 100 percent and the paperwork would be mailed. He told me that I should take algebra when possible and that he liked having me in his class. I thanked Mr. Stone and told him that the feeling was mutual.

In Lou's class, I also got a 100 percent. He asked me if it was okay to come out to the mill. I said that it would be great and I would look forward to it. I left directions on how to get there.

I was back home by nine, and Pug and Sarah were practicing. "Sounds good," I said.

"Well, how did you do?"

"100 percent on each. What do you think of that?" I asked.

"Time to celebrate with some cake and ice cream," Pug smiled. "I knew that we'd have to celebrate tonight, so I went to the ice cream parlor today!"

"Thanks, girls. This means a lot to me. Sure glad that it is over! Boy, this is good! Where did you buy the cake?"

"At Pug's bakery," said Sarah.

"Now our next big night is tomorrow," I began. "Maybe we should record all four but only release one a week. What do you think?"

Sarah thought that this was a good idea and added, "We'll see what our DJ says."

"Tomorrow's a workday, so better walk you girls home." Got double hugs and good-night kisses at the door. I got another one from Pug as I left.

She said "See you at 6:15."

Before I knew it, it was 5:30 a.m. Pug met me at the carryall with a big nose bag and thermos. We had our goodbyes and that good cup of coffee.

We picked up Greg. We had a full day of work ahead of us at the mill. All the motors were installed but will have to be shimmed for a closer tolerance with the shafts; Elmer will take care of that. We were back home by around 3:00 p.m.

Bob asked me what I thought of him coming with us tonight. I thought it would be a good idea and that everyone would feel better if he was there. "Do you feel like you would want to play the drums?"

"No, I don't think so, Don. I did play them, however, playing music isn't my bag."

"See, you later, Bob. I am going to hit the shower."

The shower felt really good, so I turned up the hot water until I couldn't stand it. I then finished it off with cold water.

I lay out on my bed and stretched another inch or two because I felt like it. I took a short nap and felt like I was ready for anything that came along.

Pug came in to check on me. She wanted to snuggle and that got me up real quick. I got the base out, and she was at the piano. We went over our songs. I didn't need any sheet music anymore. I felt real comfortable with all of our new songs. I brought out the drums and had a go on those too. It was now time to get ready for our guests.

We had fish cakes for dinner. Peg and Sarah had been preparing them. We also had corn on the cob with corn bread and vegetables. *Wow! What a meal!* Peg thought that we would have a good number of guests tonight, so we made up sixteen set-ups. Twelve people were waiting to be seated and served. Eight more came after that, and they all looked happy.

I got up and thanked everyone for being there. I let them know that they all made this night special. "All nights are special, but today, we would like to play some new songs that we have written and will be recorded tonight in a studio up in Eugene. We are all excited about it and want you folks to be the first to hear them. We are 'Louis and the Kennedys,' and here it is."

I gave a drum roll to start it off. We went over our first song, and at the end, there was a large ovation from our guests. We went into our next song, and I decided that this was enough for now. There was more clapping, and I thought it wouldn't stop. I told the audience that we had to stop now and that they could probably catch us on the radio later. We thanked them and then did "Amazing Grace." The girls sounded real good, and I played the drums as back up.

It took us a while to clean up after dinner. We needed to get ready for our Eugene trip. We decided if we left at 8:00 p.m. that we would have plenty of time to get to the studio and set everything up. We put our guitars in and away we went, "Louis and the Kennedys."

Chapter 16

The Recording Studio

We arrived at the studio as our DJ got there, Sarah's friend Kevin. He had us sit on the other side of the glass that divided the recording studio from the spectators. There were a dozen or more chairs and tables with mikes and lines all over the place. He got his show going and then came out and talked to us. Introductions were made all around. He thought our stage name would do well. We would record each song separately for now, and later on, they could be put on one album. For now separate and he suggested that we release only one at a time.

"Will try this first one and see how it does. Sometimes, it will take a week or two. Then we will give them another and so on. It may take a couple months for all four to be out there. I'm on the air, be right back."

Kevin came back and said, "Okay, what I want you to do is record one. Just the music and, of course, the lyrics. Here's your drums, get a few licks on them, Don, and see how they feel." I tried them out and they felt great.

"Hey, okay, I am ready."

"I will be right back after I set up a couple of songs with an add key," and Kevin ducked back into his booth.

We were a little nervous but mostly excited as Kevin reappeared. "Okay. Let's do it!" said Kevin. Pug was ready, and she started it off on the piano with guitars and then voice. It sounded really good. The tempo picked up. We laid down the base and got in with the drums. I think we had a good one.

When we finished, Kevin said, "Now here is the playback. Wow, it was good," Kevin said. He mentioned that he would have to make a few adjustments, and it would be ready.

He liked it! We were all smiles.

We recorded the other three, and he liked those, too, but was going to make some changes mainly in the amplification and base. "So, here's the deal," he said. "I know these are going to be hits, and I have to have some of the action."

I said, "That's fine, but let us know what you want and we can write it up and consult with our attorney. For now, we can write up an agreement between us. Like a pre-agreement. After we all sign, can you get the one on the air tonight?"

"I think that would be all right. The thing is, we don't want anyone stealing it. This happens a lot so we have to be careful how we write it up," Kevin said.

Between Kevin, Sarah, Pug, and me, we came up with a good contract that would protect the song and also leave the amount open-ended. Bob and Peg looked it over and agreed. We all signed it and made copies for us.

Kevin took the number one recording in his room, and we could hear him and the music. He told his radio audience that this is what they have been waiting for, hot off the platter, "Louis and the Kennedys."

It was about 10:30 p.m. when he played it and by 11:00 p.m., there were over one hundred calls. Of course, he could only answer about thirty of these. With that, we left Kevin and his studio. I looked back and noticed Sarah giving him a big kiss. I guess that kind of seals the deal.

Before we left town, we stopped at the Triple XXX Drive Inn. We all had root beers; I had a hamburger to go with it. Bob had two burgers, and I thought the girls had French fries.

Boy, that sure hit the spot. That was the best root beer that I ever had, tasted better than homemade.

It was Bob's treat, and we all thanked him. He said, "Just remember me when you're rich and famous." We all had a good laugh.

Bob reminded us that the wild huckleberries were ready to pick, and we should get some before the bears beat us to them. We planned on going Sunday morning, right after a breakfast.

"Don, you are invited to breakfast and to berry pick."

"Sounds good. Looking forward to it," I said.

"After Elmer shows up tomorrow, we should run him out to the mill," Bob said. "Maybe we can work a couple of hours or we can wait and see what he wants to do. We could lay things out for Monday morning and make it a real productive day."

"Can hardly wait," I said.

Chapter 17

Our Song

It was close to midnight when we got home. I told everyone that I was going to listen to our DJ for a while.

"Mom, is it okay if I stay up with Don and listen to the radio for a while?" asked Pug.

"Sure, I think it would be good."

"Thanks, Mom!"

"Good night, everyone."

"Don, isn't this the best? We can be together out here on the couch listening to our music that we just recorded!"

I turned on the radio. We sat there holding on to each other, waiting for our song. Kevin was talking and calls were still coming in for requests to play our song. Our song was playing, and it was hard to believe we had just recorded it. "Our song" sounded really good.

"Pug, I'd better walk you back now as your folks may be worrying about you."

"You should check me out first to be sure that I'm not getting fat."

"You'll have to be satisfied with the hugs for now. We will work our way into the heavy stuff after you graduate from high school. Oh, yeah, when does your school start?"

"After Labor Day and that's only two weeks away, and then after that, you start your trade school, Don."

"We can talk about this later. Let me walk you home now." At the door, I gave her a big kiss and hug.

"Good night, Don. I will bring you coffee at 7:00 a.m.?"

"Okay that's great! Good night, Pug."

Chapter 18

Saturday

I was up and dressed by 6:30 a.m. and went to the dining room. Pug got at the dining room about the same time. We sat in the dining room and talked.

"You know, Pug, you have spoiled me. There won't be all this attention when you start school, and I'll miss you."

"Don, we can still find some time to be together. Maybe you could spend some time helping me with my homework."

"Yeah, sure, I'd like that. Will you be talking algebra?"

"Yes, I will. Last year I had math. This will work out great as we could help each other out on that one."

"I'll need some algebra with the electrical classes I'll be taking at trade school. I have to leave now, Pug. I have to get my clothes together and some change so that I can go to the Laundromat. Thanks for the coffee. See you in a couple of hours."

Pug gave me a kiss before I left. I headed for the café, and Dot greeted me with a cup of coffee, and I told her that I would like the special for the day which was eggs, bacon, and waffles.

I asked her if Bruce had been in yet, and Dot let me know that he should be in soon. I looked up and there was Bruce.

"Good to see you, Don. Of course, you even more," as he gave Dot a big one.

Bruce gave his order. Dot brought his coffee and filled mine up.

"Boy, this is a good way to start the weekend. Are you working hard, Bruce?"

"Oh, sure. Keeping real busy being the crew boss. I was told to be more of a hard ass, but I think I'm getting more work out of them by being myself."

"You got that right," I said. "It's too late for you to change now, Bruce. Hope to see you all this Sunday. We have a special musical surprise for everyone."

"Okay on that. We'll see you around noon."

I left the café filled up and put my clothes in the washer. I got caught up on my comic books. There was Dick Tracy sitting at the counter of this café, talking with his chief on his wristwatch radio. Pretty neat, don't you think? Maybe would all be wearing them someday. All my clothes were done by the time I had finished Buck Rogers.

I had to wait at the barber shop. I didn't mind as it gave me a chance to reach the newspaper and catch up on all the news from the local guys. I didn't say much. Just listened and tried to absorb it all. It was my turn in the chair. I told him the short cut and shave would be good.

He commented that my hair had grown back really well and that I should probably come two times a week. This information got a good laugh from all around.

When I was done at the barber shop, I headed back home as it was going to be a busy day. I put my clothes away and counted the money in my sock. I realized that Bob had forgot to pay me. I think I would walk over there and see if he would remember.

"Hi, Don. Sit down here and let's do some business."

Pug came over with some coffee and a roll. I thanked her and let her know that she had the best coffee and rolls in the state.

"Well, Don, I have you down for four hundred dollars, plus your draws are a bonus."

"Bob, thank you very much. This is very generous of you."

"Are the banks open today?"

"Yes, they are. Ours is open until 3 p.m. I'll get down there before I meet Elmer. Thanks again, Bob."

Back at the office, I was going over my paperwork and waiting for 12:00 noon as that is when I go to town. Pug showed up at the office as someone had rang. I thought I saw someone in the store.

"Hey, Pug," I said, "that bell's a pretty good idea. That way you don't have to spend all your time over here."

"You are right. I am going over the books, and it looks as though you owe some money. How does thirty-six dollars sound? Too much?"

"Heck, no, I think that you are giving me a swell deal and you throw in all the extras."

"Well," she said, "it's kind of a trade-off, as you do a lot for me too."

I reached deep into my sock and had a lot more than thirty-six dollars in there. I still had forty-two dollars after paying Pug. I was putting my sock back and checking out the new Fender while Pug was still there.

"Don, I love you!"

"I love you, too, and respect you just as much."

We had a big kiss and a hug. I told her that I had to meet Uncle Elmer and go to the bank.

"Oh, yeah, Pug, how are we doing with our music stash?"

"We have sixty dollars and that's not bad, but when there's an attorney involved, we will need a lot more than that."

"Well, I'll stand by with more contributions when needed. Bye for now, Pug. Gotta go."

I took my bank book with me and deposited all of the check except forty dollars. I really felt rich with all that money in there.

I saw Elmer's truck. It was close to 1:00 p.m. I opened the truck door and got in and rolled the window down. I got busy rolling a smoke.

"Hey, Elmer!"

"How's it going? What's new with Bob?"

"It looks like Bob is going to join up with the coast guard. He's been talking to a recruiter in Eugene."

"I will be checking out the mill today and decide if I am coming back Monday and work for a couple of days."

We pulled up at Bob's, and he was out waiting for us. "Hey, Elmer! Come over and sit down."

Pug came out with the coffee and cinnamon rolls. Bob said that we would have some coffee and run out to the mill. "If that's okay with you, guys."

Elmer said, "I'm looking forward to seeing the progress and what was going to happen next. But first, eating one of these delicious cinnamon rolls!"

Once at the mill, Elmer gave us a few pointers on the balancing aspects of the shafts off the motors and let us know that he would be out to work Monday morning and maybe Tuesday. It would all depend on how far we got on the installation. We also need to decide where the control panels and main power would be located so that I could start the wiring.

Bob said, "It looks like Monday is going to be a big day. I look forward to getting a good start on the changeover. It is likely that there will be a shutdown in the woods due to the fire danger. However, I think we are okay there with what we are doing. Tom doesn't seem to be on the site. I will leave a note on his door to remind him to water down the area."

I had written a letter to Bob and gave it to Elmer. I let Elmer know that I would go back with him if I wasn't so busy. I asked Elmer if he wanted to stay for dinner. He said next time as he needed to get back to the cabin. He would see us Monday at the mill.

Back home, I went to the office. Pug was sitting at her desk. I asked her if she could go for a walk. She needed to let her mom know and would be back in a minute. I took the guitar out of its case. I was doing some chords when Pug came in.

"After our walk, maybe we could play some music together," she said.

We walked to the ice cream parlor and sat on the bench outside, enjoying our cones. We talked about school, music, and work mostly. We decided to take back some ice cream so we could have some tonight and possibly with pie as we were picking berries tomorrow.

We went through some gospels together with just piano and my base with us singing. I thought it sounded pretty good. We thought that asking Sarah to listen to us would give us some good feedback. Pug thought that we should play the song we had just been going through at dinner and see if the guests like it.

We continued to practice and go over the song a few times more, making changes as we went along. I thought that we could play this song and the one that is playing on the radio. I said that I had to go and help with dinner.

"Don, don't be afraid of me, come here," Pug responded.

There she goes, I was afraid that I have fallen for her. I was sure that it was only puppy love as I kept forgetting that I was only fourteen, but everyone else thought that I was eighteen. Still, eighteen was a long way from having responsibilities.

It was only 3:30 p.m. and I think I would take a shower. Boy, how I loved that shower. We never had a shower at home, only a bath tub. I turned up the hot water and really enjoyed it. I laid out on my bed and did some stretching. I fell asleep for about fifteen minutes.

When I woke up, Pug was there. I told her that I was resting up from our big night at the dinner musical and then our radio station in Eugene.

"Don, we were fortunate to have all this going on in our lives," Pug said.

"Yes," I said. "I'm very thankful, especially with you in my life."

We had a quick kiss and hug. Then we went to get ready for our guests. I told her it seemed like there were always different people at dinner and not very many repeats.

"Yes, there a lot of them are transients on their way to California or up to Portland or Seattle. The people that stay have usually found some kind of work mainly in the woods. Since it is Saturday, there probably won't be as many people showing up, so only make eighteen set-ups."

Chapter 19

Becoming Popular

I made eighteen set-ups. Just as I finished setting up my drums and base, I noticed that people were starting to show up. I began serving them some good home-made, home-grown vegetable soup with corn bread and butter, plus there was a pitcher of milk at the long table.

We had served about ten guests when Peg read from Psalms and said a prayer of thanks. We began singing "Amazing Grace" and "Sentimental Journey." Sarah was on the guitar, Pug on the piano, and me on the drums.

Another six guests arrived, and we served them. I put out more milk along with some more corn bread. Peg did more reading from Psalms and a prayer of thanks.

I told our guests how welcome they were and that we had a couple of new songs that we would like to try out on them from our group, "Louis and the Kennedys." I did a drum roll and said, "Let's hit it."

We played the one spiritual that we had worked on and got a large ovation. I thanked them and we went to our hit that was on the radio. People were standing up, clapping, and yelling "*More!*" We went through our song one more time and bowed and thanked them very much.

We sat down to eat. Pug said that she was looking forward to the radio tonight. I said that I also was looking forward to it as it is our big night out on the air waves.

After cleaning up the dining room, we decided to practice our music and we also worked on a new song. It was a mixture of soul, rhythmic blues, and rock-a-billy.

Pug went to the house and said that she would be back in a few minutes. I was enjoying my guitar. I realized that it fits me and I was getting a lot better with it. I looked up and there was Pug with some berry pie and ice cream.

"Wow, where did you get that pie?" I asked.

"Sarah and I made a couple of pies. We picked the berries this morning. Logan berries right out of our garden."

We sat at a table in the dining room and enjoyed that pie and ice cream. Pug held my hand and told me how much she loved me. She also said that we both had special talents with music and that she was sure that we would make it big. If we didn't, then we still had each other.

"You are right in what you said. I'll add that our talents don't stop at music. We are both good workers and follow through with our projects. In other words, the world is our oyster. We can accomplish anything we set our minds to."

We had finished our pie and moved to the couch to listen to Kevin, our favorite DJ, as it was almost 9:00 p.m. We got in on the local news. There was talk about shutting down the woods or their being restrictions which would affect the owl shift. There were some ads read by Kevin; it sounded like him doing the ads as that's how he makes his money. Kevin then said, "Well, boys and girls, this is what you've been waiting for, Louis and the Kennedys!"

"It really sounds good, doesn't it, Pug?"

"Yes, I could hear it over and over again! I think we should release our next one in a week or two. I will have Sarah check with Kevin. Did you hear that, Don? Another request for our song. I think we should release another one and get them on a label, like a record company. We can talk to Sarah about it at breakfast. In the meantime, we will have to be patient."

I said that we were pretty good with being patient. I knew it will work out. "When we start getting money from the records, what do you plan on doing with it?"

"Well, you know it won't be too much as it has to be split up. There are four of us and there is the record company. I think mine will go into saving and hold out enough for a car."

"That's about what I will do, buy a pick up and the rest into saving and get your dad's mill in operation again as that is the real bread winner."

We had been listening to the radio now for a half an hour. There had been over thirty requests for our song. We sat there until 10:30 p.m. I told Pug that I would walk her home.

"Don, with you in my life, I've never felt so happy. I look forward to our next day together," said Pug.

"I feel the same way, Pug, and write that some of that down. Good night and I will see you in the morning."

I put the drums away and picked up my guitar. *I guess it's okay to call it mine* I thought. I played it for about an hour. It felt like a part of me now.

Chapter 20

Bear!

I hit the sack, and before I knew it, another day was beginning. I took a shower and got dressed for breakfast at the Kennedy's. Afterward, we were going berry picking.

Breakfast at the Kennedy's was a real event. A lot better food and fun than the café. When it was over, we all got in the carryall with our buckets, containers, and drinking water.

We drove up a logging road and went past the mill up higher than we had picked before. A lot of people called these huckleberries or high-altitude blueberries. Bob wanted us all to be within earshot of each other. There will be bear foraging and putting on lots of fat for the winter.

We parked at an old cold deck. We walked a short distance to an area with berry bushes everywhere. The bear signs were evident too.

Within an hour, Pug and I had our buckets full. Pug had been picking close to me. I figured it was because I had the equalizer on me (my hatchet). Not sure about fighting off a bear with it, but he would have a headache.

At the carryall, we poured our berries into a large container. We found some bushes with larger berries. Within a half an hour, we were filled up again. Pug had to let everyone know that we had just finished our second fill up. After emptying our berries, we decided to take a break.

All of a sudden, Peg, Sarah, and Bob were yelling and running toward us with a large bear right behind them!

Pug and I stood our ground and waved our arms and yelled, as the others joined us and did the same. The bear put the brakes on all four, turned a 180, and took off like a shot.

We jumped in the carryall, thankful the bear turned and for the fresh berry pie we would enjoy tonight.

Chapter 21

Radio Time

It was noon and here some people came, then more people. They just kept coming in. We must have served around sixteen when Peg read some verses out of Psalms, and everyone said a prayer of thanks. Peg had set the prayers on the tables earlier. I welcomed everyone, and we began playing some spiritual songs. As we played, Bruce, Greg, and a few more guests showed up. Pug and Sarah sang another song, and I took over the serving. After I served everyone, Pug led another prayer of thanks.

I welcomed everyone again and let them know Louis and the Kennedys had some new songs coming out, and they would be the first to hear them. With that, I gave them a drumroll, and we played our first song. It was a hit!

We rolled right into our second song, which hadn't been recorded yet, and it was even better. Maybe the people were hungry for music as much as food.

After serving up our rendition of "Sentimental Journey," and it took a while for everyone to calm down.

"Well," I said, "thank you, thank you very much," to more clapping and hollering. Peg and I finally sat down and ate with our friends.

"You guys are really the best," said Dot. "I've seen a lot of shows in San Francisco and Los Angeles, and you guys are as good as any of them."

"We're not getting our hopes that high," said Pug, "but you can hear us on AM radio out of Eugene. We went up there one night and recorded some of our songs."

"You guys should do some more appearances," said Dot. "You could hit Seattle, for starters."

I said that we couldn't go anywhere until the mill was up and running. It was our bread and butter. We decided to all go out for ice cream. Peg and I had single cones, and everyone else got double cones. It came out to about ninety cents, and it was my treat. I also ordered a double-wrapped quart to take home for thirty-five cents.

I walked home with Peg, Pug, and Sarah and put everything away except for the drum set and guitar. We played and tweaked one of our new songs until Pug had to run home and help with the berries. That gave me a chance to shower up and straighten up my desk.

Here came Pug, and it looked like she brought some dessert. Berry pie and ice cream!

"Don," she said, "these are the berries we picked this morning. Couldn't be fresher."

"Looks like you've already had a piece," I said. "Want to split another one with me?"

"Oh, no, Don. That might get my spare tire started. Let's sit on the couch and listen to some music. Maybe our DJ Kevin is on."

DJ Kevin wasn't on. We just missed *Green Hornet*, but *Inner Sanctum* was on, starring Doc and Reggie. There goes that squeaking door, boy, that always sent shivers up my spine.

Nine o'clock came, and DJ Kevin came on. He would be on all night. We all sat around the radio, hoping to hear our song.

"Here he is, Pug!" I said.

"Good evening, ladies and gentlemen, also you girls and boys! I have special treats for everyone tonight. The first twenty callers will get tickets to the concert on the twenty-fourth of September at Harmony Hall, where you will dig some new sounds!"

His phone was jammed. But we didn't care because he played our song. We thought it sounded great! "Pug," I said, "find out about the concert. We should try and play there if there's room for us.

"I'll go to the house and talk to Sarah and Mom about it to see if it's okay. You should try and call him now."

We all walked over to the house. It took a few calls to get through. Sarah ended up doing the talking. She let him know that we were all here and available on the twenty-fourth.

He was glad that we called and that he had room for us. We could jazz up the program and, no doubt, bring people in. He played our song again.

"Here's another surprise for my favorite listeners. Louis and the Kennedys will be there on the twenty-fourth! Buy those tickets ASAP before they're sold out!"

I said good night to everyone, and Pug walked me to the door. She gave me a good night kiss and told me she would call me at ten to six.

Morning came quickly, and Pug and I were at the carry all saying our goodbyes. I was having some of that good coffee when Bob showed up. We picked up Greg: at the mill before seven, and we got a lot done by lunchtime. I told the boss we would need some conduit and fittings because I couldn't make all the old stuff work. Also a pipe bender.

I wanted everything to look good as well as being functional. Bob said he would place an order after lunch and get to the supplier by the afternoon. The supplier was up in Eugene.

"Maybe you could go up there and take what you need," the boss said, "and tell your uncle we're ready for him tomorrow or Wednesday. That way, by Thursday or Friday, Greg and I will move the donkey to a new show, and we'll have the faller come in."

We had everything laid out and measured up, with a list of needed materials by one-thirty. After dropping off Greg and arriving at home, the boss gave me some cash and his checkbook. He told me where the supplier was, and he would call ahead of time and let them know I was representing him.

I gave Pug a kiss. She filled my thermos with fresh coffee and told me she would keep her base radio station on standby and let me know to do the same.

Chapter 22

Surprise Visit

Well, I was off, with plenty of gas and a full thermos! I was excited to be driving the carry all, but I didn't let it show! I made it to the supplier before three, and I got everything I needed. I even got a pipe bender "to keep." I drove to Sutherlin, pulled up to the cabin, and parked by the Model A, and there was Bob under the hood.

"What do you want?" he hollered. "We're not buying anything. Oh my gosh, it's you, Don!"

Bob rushed toward me and gave me a big bear hug. "Boy, did you surprise me! Where did you steal this carry all? Hope you have a license or they'll haul you off to jail for sure!"

Just then, Elmer walked in from the garden. We all sat down on some stumps, and Bob filled me in on what was going on. He signed up for the coast guard and would be taking a train to Los Angeles, then San Diego for boot camp. After that, back east somewhere.

It looked like neither of us had to start school in Edmunds, Washington. It was a real bummer to not be together, but we could all do our own thing and be successful.

"Oh, yeah!" Bob said. "That girl who has been chasing me decided to go back to Bremerton. I'm sure she'll hook some lucky sailor."

We laughed and promised to send each other letters. I wasn't going anywhere, of course. I planned to stay in Roseburg as long as possible. I started trade school in a few weeks and would continue working for the Kennedy Logging Company, which paid okay and provided room and board.

"You've been hitting the feedbag," he said.

"They feed me real good," I said, "apple pie and cinnamon rolls every day. But I've been keeping up with my hatchet throwing, so I can still handle anything that comes my way."

"Oh, yeah?" Elmer said. "How about you hit that stump over there?"

He pointed to a stump about fifteen feet away. I grabbed my hatchet and belt from the carry all, strapped it on, then came back to where I was sitting. I unbuckled the sheath and turned my back to it.

"Tell me when," I told Bob.

At his signal, I turned and drew the hatchet, then flung it into the stump.

"How the heck did you do that?" Bob gasped.

"You were too close," Elmer said. "Walk away from it about ten more feet."

I retrieved the hatchet and did the trick again. That got them clapping.

"Look at you," Bob said. "You grew up a lot this summer, you know. You're doing a man's job now. What do you think, Elmer?"

"You said it all, Bob," he said.

I told Bob I knew he'd do well in the coast guard, and Elmer that the mill was ready to hire him whenever he was. Before I left, we ate the three cinnamon rolls Pug had put in my nose bag. I said my goodbyes and headed down the road.

Chapter 23

Protector

I got home as everyone was finishing dinner. Before I had what was left of the spaghetti with venison and toast, I thanked Pug for the coffee and rolls by pulling her into my office and giving her a big kiss.

The spaghetti was good. Pug's mom let that sauce cook all day, and it tasted great with venison and garlic bread. Pug had helped a lot of guests at the Salvation Army that day.

"We didn't play any of our music since you weren't around," she said, "but we still did some gospel and blues."

I told her I'm sure it was real good without me, and we talked about our big gig coming up on the twenty-fourth. We wondered how the stage would be set up. There had to be a piano, but we wondered if we would have to bring the drum set.

She walked back to the house to get some dessert, and I went outside to throw my hatchet a bit before the sun went down. I'm glad I did because a shady-looking fellow was standing in the alley between the cabin and the house.

I asked if he was looking for something. "My pet elephant got away. I'm just up here looking for him."

I didn't care for his smartass remark, so I asked him his name, and when he didn't give it, I told him he wasn't welcome here. I tossed the ax at the target stump to make a point. He left pretty quickly. By the time I retrieved the hatchet and threw it again, he was farther away and still in a hurry.

Pug was standing in the doorway with the ice cream and pie. "You put on a good show, Don. He believed you. I'm so glad you protected me."

I smiled. "Our real protector is God," I said. "He put me here to help you, and he put you here as my angel, Pug." She told me I was good with words. We sat down at the table and talked until well after the ice cream had melted. DJ Kevin came on the radio and played our song again.

We talked about getting an attorney to protect our songs. Now that we were getting popular, someone was bound to steal our music if they could get away with it.

We wondered if we would have to go farther than Eugene to find one. Dot, Bruce's friend, seemed to know her way around music. She probably had some information.

"Life sure is exciting, Don," Pug said.

It is when you can keep up with it, I told her, or you're a few steps ahead. We wrote down a few lyrics on a notepad before it was time to turn in.

My big day left me feeling exhausted, but I still walked Pug home. I kept my hand on my hatchet the whole walk there and back, but there was no sign of the fellow looking for his elephant.

Chapter 24

Progress

We had a productive day at the mill. Elmer got in by eight and got the motors set up. We called it a day at three and asked Bob if we could install a couple of lights in the alley. He also told me he would call the police and ask them to patrol the alley once in a while. We were sure that the mill would be ready for the inspector by Thursday or Friday. I stopped by the police and gave a description of the trespasser. When I got home, I used some lights and wiring I had purchased for the mill and began setting up the outdoor lighting. I didn't get as much done as I wanted, but I got one light on a pole by the shed and another by the spot where we parked the carry all. We all appreciated the extra light when night fell.

I took a hot shower and dressed for dinner at the Salvation Army. Pug was waiting for me with a kiss. We reached the Salvation Army in ten minutes. People were already there, so I finished setting the tables quickly and brought out a pitcher of milk. By the time I was bringing out the drum set, I realized I was bone tired. I told Pug, and she said she'd fill in for me.

We had served ten dinners and said a prayer of thanks, and suddenly, I got a second wind. While the band was playing, I hopped on the drum set, then switched to bass in the next song. I loved that guitar. Something about the prayer and the music did it for me.

After Pug, Sarah, and I ate our dinner, we talked about turning the Lord's Prayer into a song. Three hours later, we had the fundamentals worked out. Pug and Sarah's voices sounded great together, and I started with some light drumming that switched to bass at the end.

We felt good about it and decided to play it tomorrow. We talked about what other Bible verses we could turn into songs. Peg said she could think about a dozen that would go well with our music. We could release our religious material separately than other songs. We still needed to talk to Dot about finding an attorney to protect our songs.

I hoped my work on the mill wouldn't cut into the time we would need to work with our attorney. Both were taking a lot of effort. We had to make sure this attorney was 100 percent with our interests. We had to pay him ourselves and get our second song on the radio before our first song started slipping. I walked the girls back to their house and went to bed. Another long day was ahead of me.

Pug was there at ten to six with a goodbye kiss. The day was off to a good start. I got into the carry all with my coffee filled, and Bob got in the truck. We reached the mill, and Tom was hosing the whole place down. We did more work on the motors, and by nine-thirty, we had finished up the conduits.

We took a coffee break, and I gave Tom one of my cinnamon rolls. That put a smile on his face. A roll and a coffee made for a good break.

After the break, I went up to the power company and let them know we were ready for them, and they told me they'd be there Thursday or Friday. I thought it would be a good time for Lou to come over and take a look at the work. He said he would stop by sometime during the week. I hoped he would show up soon.

I looked over at all the machinery to make sure the connections were good and the panels were in place. I cleaned and wiped down everything and marked them. I asked Tom if anyone had been around to look at the wiring, and he said no.

I pushed the sawdust pile a good twenty feet away from the mill and searched the place for anything that would start a fire. Sure enough, there was a large coal burning up the sawdust.

That gave Tom something to do. He sprayed it down with the hose, then went over everything one more time. He liked how everything looked when it was wet. He thought it made everything look brand new.

I was topping off the gas in the carry all, and here came Lou. "Hey, Don, it looks like you're just about done."

"I think I am. Right now, I'm just waiting on more service and an inspection."

"Boy, you don't mess around. Where's the boss?"

Tom came out and said that when the owner wasn't around, I was boss. I told Lou that Tom was my right-hand man and caretaker. Lou looked around the mill and liked what he saw. He wanted to turn the motors on.

"I'm not sure about that," I told him, "I don't think there's enough voltage yet."

"Sure, there is, Don. All we have to do is some jumping and we can run one system, one at a time."

Lou went to his truck and returned with some a voltage tester and some jumper leads. At the master control panel, he jumped 220 to the number 1 control box, flipped it on. It read 220 and he said clear. Everything looked okay. I decided to test the headsaw. It ran. Wow, was it ever smooth and quiet.

"Okay," said Lou, "turn it off."

Tom said it was hard for him to believe it ran so smooth. I told him my uncle, a machinist, set it and supervised us when necessary. We tested the other saws, and they were also smooth and quiet. It was exciting to see them work.

Bob was spending the next few days logging. We hoped to have logs in the pond, ready to cut, by next Wednesday. I told Lou maybe he could come back when it was operating. I was concerned about the load on the headsaw.

"I wouldn't worry about it, Don," Lou said. "That motor on 220 on the other mill cut good-sized logs. Probably bigger logs than the ones you're going to get. However, that first log you run through will let us know for sure." Before Lou left, he told us there's no reason why we wouldn't pass inspection.

That was a relief.

"If you have trouble, tell him I oversaw the whole operation, and give him my card," Lou said, handing me his business card. I thanked him and told him how much his help meant to me.

I turned off the electrical box and told Tom that he was the man I was waiting for. He was the electrical instructor, and he taught me everything I knew. I told him the power company would be here in the morning, and that they should know what to do.

On the way home, I stopped by Bob's and told him about the mill, and he told me about his day. We talked about our plans for the next morning and hoped the power company would show up. "Wait until you hear the motors," I told him, "they're really sweet."

I made it home and showered and found some time to stretch out on my bed. It wasn't long before Pug found me and got me to help with the serving.

Dinner smelled great. It was a stew made of venison and vegetables from the garden, served with corn bread. I set out the usual jug of milk and some water. There were fifteen guests that night.

We played "Sentimental Journey" and our new rendition of the Lord's Prayer. They loved it. We sat down to our dinner, and I was sure to grab some extra corn bread. We talked and agreed that Louis and the Kennedys should meet up on Saturday or Sunday, when we had word about an attorney.

After cleaning up the dining area, we practiced our songs. We had five now, counting our version of the Lord's Prayer. We thought it would be a good idea to do a few more spirituals but to play them more like country or rock. People were ready for that new sound.

We played another hour and went back to the house. It wasn't quite dark, but I turned on the flood light I had installed the night before and told Pug I would wire it up to the house so we could turn it on or off there.

There was always a lot to do, but it kept me focused. We had dessert. Pug made some cake. I told her it was her best ever and asked how she did it.

"Oh, it's just the regular stuff, but I added more TLC."

We talked about other projects that could be done. We turned on the radio and heard our song again. DJ Kevin said that he would be playing another Louis and the Kennedys song on Saturday.

"I guess Sarah called him and told him it would be a good time to drop our new song," Pug said with a smile. It was good to have the support of friends.

I gave Pug a flashlight she could carry after dark. It was heavy, and it threw light a good block away. It also looked kind of like a weapon. I walked her back to her house with the new flashlight and kissed her good night.

I had a long, hard day ahead of me because I was helping Bob at the log site. Pug met me at the truck first thing in the morning with a hug, coffee, and my nose bag (lunchbox).

Bob showed up a little after I did, and I told him I would meet him at the landing, where we would get the trailer with the wood. It was good and light when we got to the landing. I backed in and waited for Bob, who operated the loader.

Bob had Greg helping him. He started the loader, and I watched him so I could learn to do it. Anyway, he had my trailer off in no time, and Greg was setting his first chocker. Bob set it on the trailer and kept it up until I was loaded, then put on the binders. "Don't forget to retighten!" Bob yelled.

I gave him a thumbs up and tightened the load before getting on the highway. By seven-thirty, we reached the mill pond. Tom was there to help unload and get the trailer back on.

"Boy, those are some big ones!" he said.

I told him we would be back before nine and that we could take a break. While I was there, I refilled the truck's gas tank and my coffee cup and hit the road.

Bob had me loaded up again in no time, and we were back at the pond at nine. Tom and I got everything unloaded, and we ate cinnamon rolls. I think Tom was going to get used to those rolls.

I took a third trip to the landing, where workers had stacked up a lot of logs. Bob loaded me up, and away I went with load number three. I wondered if we would get six that day. By eleven-thirty, we were on four.

We had a quick lunch. I ate a good sandwich, which probably had some of that stew meat. We hauled in six loads, but it was past four when we unloaded the last one. Tom helped me get the trailer back on, and I asked him if he'd seen the power company guys. He hadn't seen anyone but me and those logs.

Tom told me he would keep the outside lights on, in case anyone got an ideas about our logs. It was a good idea. I said I would see him at seven the next morning.

I made it back to the house in time for a shower. But I barely got to stretch out on the bed because it was dinner time.

It all went well. We had more success with the music. Tomorrow would be the big day. The big inspection.

Chapter 25

The Big Inspection

We got another load of logs to the pond by seven-thirty.

"We might have too many logs," Tom said.

"Oh, come on," I told him, "you can push them around and stack them and we're only half full."

I tacked Lou's card on our electrical permit. We hoped everyone would show up that day. I drove out for another load and came back at nine. Tom and I had a cinnamon roll break. "You deserve it," I told him.

"You're right there, Don."

I filled up my coffee cup, and off I went. I was back with load number three before eleven. I had a quick turnaround, was back with more by twelve-thirty. I gassed up the truck, checked oil and water, ate my sandwich, and drove back to the landing.

Once there, I positioned the truck and asked Bob if I couldn't try to load some more logs. I did well on the trailer, but I was having trouble getting the logs on right.

"Take your time," Bob said, "and with a lot of practice, you'll make it. But let me finish with the loading today."

I saw a lot of logs left. I told Bob that another four or five loads might fill up the pond.

"We're doing five loads, Don. I don't want any breakdowns, so just slow down and take it steady. I doubt if we'll have a go from the state inspection until next week."

I went back to the mill with load four. Back at the mill, I ran the loader to put my trailer where it belonged. I asked Tom what he thought of the gas engine on the loader.

"I really like it," Tom said. "Hope we don't change it over."

It was a Ford 60HP V8 engine. The best little engine Ford made. Tom kept it well-maintained. He changed the oil, tuned it up, etc. It was up to Bob if we changed it or not, but I put in the good word. Tom thought it would take two or three more loads to fill the pond. I took the log pole and did my best to make some room. I was still going for five. Maybe six, like the day before.

I made it back to the landing, and Bob loaded me up. I was back at the mill before two. Tom said there wasn't room for a sixth load, but I wasn't so sure. "Make some room," I said. We dumped the fifth load in, and it looked like Tom was right. A few logs weren't floating, but it was a pretty sight.

I made it back to the house at four and gave the truck a good washing. I just finished when Bob rolled in. I gave the carry all a quick rinse too. Bob thanked me for all the extra work I was doing and was happy that we got all of the logs in.

I told him the pond was full, and it sure looked good. Bob said there was probably enough logs on the cold deck and in the draw for another fourteen loads.

"Do you want to run out to the mill with me, Don?" I told him sure. He gave me my draw, twenty dollars.

"Hope that's enough." It was. I thanked him.

We got back to the mill, and there was Tom. He worked while I was gone, running from log to log, and he got all of them floating. I said, "Hey there, Tom, it looks like we could get another load in there."

"Oh, no! Oh, no!" Tom replied.

Bob told him the pond looked nice, and he gave him his pay. Bob took a look at the permit I left at the mill and smiled.

"They signed it off! I guess Lou's card helped," he said. "Hey, Tom. It looks like the inspector got in without you seeing him. The job is bought off! Boy, I feel good now. All we need is more power."

He told Tom he was doing a good job and to keep the area wet over the weekend.

"Let's go home, Don, and feed the hungry," he said.

"Talk about being hungry," I said, "when are you going hunting? Deer season opened up in two weeks, and then came the October elk season."

"You can come with me," he said. "We could get more meat to pack out the two of us. Any elk herds around here?"

It was about fifty miles to the Cascade herd and about the same distance for the Roosevelt herd. We talked about getting zeroed in on a gun, maybe on Sunday. It would be a good time to find where the deer are and do some target shooting. He would set me up with a rifle. I was excited.

I showered, and then I stretched out on the bed. I swear I grew an inch. I heard a lot of popping and felt some pulling going on. Next thing I knew, Pug was giving me kissing. I laughed and told her they were nice. They didn't bother me as much as they used to.

"Come on, Don," she said. "Let's get ready for our guests."

Well, we did that and did the whole thing with Pegs' prayers and our music with some very good soup and dinner rolls. I told Sarah and Peg that I would like to have a meeting Sunday afternoon or evening. We all agreed on six o'clock in the evening.

After cleaning the dining room, we practiced music until eight. Then Pug and I walked over to the house and got some dessert. It was the kind of chocolate cake I liked so much. We sat there, enjoying the cake and a good conversation. We moved to the couch and turned on the radio. There was our DJ friend, Kevin. Boy, was he a good talker. He was getting everyone warmed up for tomorrow night. He had a brand-new hit, just recorded, and we would be the first to hear it.

"Do you think it's our number two song?" Pug asked.

"I think it is," said Sarah.

It would be the right time, while our first song was still in the top ten. We listened to the radio for an hour. I walked Pug home. She had the flashlight I gave her. It worked really well.

I dropped her off at her house, then walked back through the alley. As I was wondering if a patrol car ever came through, one pulled up to me. I said hello to him, and he told me that the flood light was helping with security. I told him I appreciated his extra surveillance and asked if he had seen any unusual people around there at night.

"No, I think you have them scared," he said.

The officer's name was Officer Kevin, but he told me to knock off the "officer" handle, unless I was around the station, before he drove away. Another Kevin. It was good to have a friend at the police station.

Chapter 26

Weekend

I hit the sack, and before I knew it, there was Pug with a thermos of coffee. I thanked her for the coffee. She had a certain knack for making everything feel good. Sadly, I couldn't stay with her long. I had to run off to do my laundry and get a haircut. I kissed her goodbye and told her I'd see her in a couple of hours.

At the Laundromat, I checked out the new Buck Rogers comic book. Buck and his girlfriend were going to the moon for a two-week stay to check out mining operation. I got so caught up in it that I almost forgot to come back to earth and do the drying.

After doing my laundry, I met Bruce and Dot at the cafe. Bruce had a grin on his face, so I asked him what was new.

He managed to work every day without going to the owl shift and save up enough to buy his own pickup. It was a 1940 Ford with low mileage with an 85HP V8 engine with three-speed and an over-drive. It even looked new. I told him it sounded pretty good and that he probably didn't have to double-clutch it.

"Good one, Don!" he said.

I told him I was thinking about getting that same truck. But a good pickup would have to wait because of my music venture. I wasn't sure how much the attorney would charge.

Dot told me she would talk to the attorney that afternoon. I grinned when she said the attorney she had in mind already knew about us.

Apparently, DJ Kevin had sent our song to a friend in San Francisco. I thanked her for all of her help. I paid the seventy-five cent bill for our breakfast and headed to the barber.

"Hi, Don," the barber said, "how they hanging?"

I laughed. That was a new one. While I waited for my turn, I chatted with the other men. They were talking about how it was a dry year. If the rain didn't come soon, the woods would be closed for logging and deer hunting. But there was a front coming in from the ocean that was supposed to hit on Monday.

When it was my turn, I told the barber to give me the works because I had a big week ahead of me.

"Why is it big?" the barber asked.

I told him I heard that some people from Alaska and Seattle were moving south to find a warmer climate. They would probably be coming through the Armory for dinner. Hopefully, they'd find their way farther south, like San Francisco. The guys laughed at that one.

The barber asked me if I could come in twice a week, and I told him I didn't think he could do a half-job.

"But I've been putting hair grow in your lather," he said.

He finished up, and I got home at about ten. I plucked at my bass, and it sounded out of tune. I couldn't get the strings adjusted right, so I replaced them. It wasn't long before it sounded as good as new.

Pug came in, and we started practicing our music. She strummed the guitar and made a face.

"It sounds different. You changed the strings."

I didn't know why it bothered her, so I changed the topic. I asked her if it would be a good idea if we mailed ourselves a recording of our music for copyright purposes. She thought so. We practiced until it was almost time for me to meet up with Bob about the mill. I wished I could stay with Pug longer. I told her I felt like I loved her more every day. We had a light lunch of PBJ sandwiches, and I kissed her goodbye.

I got in the truck and rolled up a smoke. Elmer showed up after a few minutes.

"I have some news for you," he said.

He sounded serious. I asked him what was going on.

"Bob will be leaving on the eight a.m. train in Eugene. I will drive him up there, and after that, I'll show up at the mill. I'll try to get a ride up there in the morning and then ride with you back to the mill."

I figured that wasn't the only thing going on, so I asked what else was new.

"Nothing with me. It's just Bob is leaving quietly to get away from some drama. The two sisters are fighting over him. No one but us knows that he's going away on Monday. I think he wants you to use the car while he's gone, or you can just leave it with me if you want."

Then, he handed me a letter. It was from my mom. She said she was moving to Ballard and Dad was staying in Bremerton so he didn't have too far to commute to his work. I hoped they would get along better that way.

We drove to the wood shed at Bob's, and there he was sitting at the picnic table.

"Good to see you, Elmer!" Bob said. "Let's get this meeting going. Of course, we should get some rolls and coffee."

The girls came out with the rolls and coffee, but Pug also had a notebook and a pencil. After finishing up our snack, Bob started the meeting. Pug read the minutes of the meeting last Saturday. We had a lot of new things to discuss since then.

I brought up that we passed the electrical inspection, but we still weren't hooked up with more power. The good news was that the motors were all singing, and they seemed well-balanced. Bob added that the mill pond was full of logs, and they were cold-decking more logs at the show.

"If there's nothing else," Bob said, "let's close the meeting so we can talk."

We got more coffee and rolls, and Elmer told Pug that she should open a bakery in town.

"I don't know about that," said Bob as he began munching on a roll. "Then we'd have to buy these."

I asked Bob if there was a way I could get a ride to Eugene on Monday morning to see off my brother. I told him he was leaving on the 8:00 a.m. train to boot camp. He told me I could take the carry all up there, and he could drive the car to the logging show.

Elmer thanked Pug for the rolls and coffee and said he would see us on Monday. I asked Bob if he was still on for the morning hike. We wanted to get an early start, around six, with our rifles. We decided we might as well look at the guns we would use. We went into a house, and Bob showed me the 270 Remington he liked. He told me he never missed with it.

I liked the Winchester 30/30. It had a lever action and buck-horn sights. Bob said it was good up to 150 yards, but it was best for 100. He also had a 30/40, which packed some real power, and was good for 200 yards. I told Bob I like the 30/30 the most.

I made it to the Armory in time to help with dinner. There was a pretty good turnout for a Saturday. Word must have been getting out that we were the place for good food and good music!

After dinner, Pug and I walked up to the overlook. It was nice to just sit there with her and look out over the valley and see the distant mountains. We got some ice cream and watched the sunset from a bench. We brought back a quart for everyone at the house.

When we got home, we practiced our music some more. Sarah and Peg showed up after about an hour. We played and rearranged the gospel songs we had been playing. We talked about getting twelve down so we could record them together on a different label.

It was time to turn on our favorite DJ.

"Here's that surprise I've been saving for you! Another hit from Louis and the Kennedys!"

We cheered, then made ourselves be quiet as the song played. I held Pug's hand, feeling almost as proud as I did when I heard our first song. We were off to a good start.

"Was that us?" Sarah said, laughing. "Gosh, we sounded so good."

"I'm sure DJ Kevin's going to send this one to his friend in San Fran, too," said Pug.

I started feeling a little more humble. This music venture would take hard work before it paid off. I said we should enjoy this while we could, but we shouldn't get bigger than our pants. Before I knew it, bedtime came. I said goodbye to Pug at the door, with an extra hug and kiss.

I met up with Bob at ten to six, and we took off with our rifles, coffee, and rolls. Within an hour, we reached high country. We stopped at a knoll that had been logged off within the last five years, and we had a 360 degree view of the land around us.

We set up our spots and watched the brush. A half an hour later, some brush moved. I pointed it out to Bob with a big grin. "That's something," he said. "But I don't see any antlers."

He wanted to follow it some and see if he could get a better look. Two does stepped out into the open. My heart began to thump. Something looked like it was following them. Bob was drawing closer. Maybe he would spook them and send them my way!

The animal came out of the brush. It looked like a two-point buck to me. I held my rifle tight and waited, hoping it would move closer to me. I guessed it was still three or four hundred yards away.

I smiled as another one, bigger, showed up, not too far from the first group. He was holding back, and I couldn't see him entirely. But judging by his size, he was maybe a four-point buck. He was a smart one. He was staying away from the clearing.

Bob crept back to where I was, and I told him about what I saw and gave him a signal about a good position. By the time Bob got back down the knoll, the deer had moved on, and I lost sight of them. But they were a bit closer now. They must have been only about two hundred yards away.

Bob checked in with me again, and I signaled where the deer had gone. We took a coffee break. Bob said he liked this area, but there was another place he wanted to check out too. It was another logged out area with plenty of brush. I went along with him. It wasn't long before we arrived.

The new spot had a 180-degree view, about a half-mile deep. Bob suggested I slowly go deep into the tree line and then work my way toward the clearing. I set out. One hand was on my hatchet, in case a bear or lion leaped out at me. After a half-hour, I felt like I was in the center of the trees.

There were a lot of deer trails. I got out my compass and did some readings, then kept walking. I found an area of about two acres, with some apple and pear trees and remnants of a cabin. I picked up a few interesting artifacts scattered on the ground. I would have liked to stay there longer, but Bob was at the top of the tree line, waiting for me.

I made it back and saw him on a hill. I signaled to him with a piece of glass I found at the homestead. He saw me, and he waved me to come back. It took me awhile to reach him. It was a good workout.

He told me I'd scared up three deer. One of them was a good-sized buck, a four or five-pointer. I told him about the cabin and the fruit trees and all of the deer signs.

"By the way, Don," Bob said, "these deer were within one hundred yards. We should come back next week when there isn't a fire danger."

I remembered that we weren't even supposed to be up there. We got out of the woods before we ran into any rangers. We stopped by the mill before we returned home to make sure the area was wetted down.

I told Bob about getting an engine for the mill's water pump, in case the electric motor broke down. "Good thinking," Bob said. "Plus, it'll make Tom happy. He likes those engines. Also, we can change the off-loader at the pond to a motor sometime."

We pulled up to the mill, and there was Tom out on the pond. It looked like he made more room. I topped off the carry all at the gas pump and checked the water and brake fluid.

Bob inspected the mill perimeter, making sure everything was damp. I noticed the sawdust pile looked drier than I liked.

Hopefully, Bob would drill into Tom's head how important it was to keep everything wet, especially because of how dry the woods were. As we left the mill, I saw Tom spraying everything down again.

"Good thing, we filled that pond before the dry spell," Bob said.

When we got back home, I laid out the artifacts from the old homestead on the picnic table. The girls came out to see what we brought back. They had a good time of it as I told them about how I saw part of an old chimney, a well, and the orchard. It might have dated back to the 1880s.

I looked forward to going back to hunt and explore the area next weekend.

About the Author

The author's life history had many adventures, included raising a family, no time to think about writing. He had many friends telling him to "write that down," which he finally did, after four years and two thousand printed pages. He was on his own at fourteen, fighting forest fires in Oregon State, setting chuckers for logging companies, also lumber mill work. He expanded his horizons by attending night school, followed by a high school diploma which he was very proud of. He also impressed Uncle Sam as he sent him a draft notice. He joined the US Air Force where more schools were required. His favorite one was California school of aeronautics. After years of keeping them flying, he went back to civilian life, his employment with Douglas experimental flight testing at Edwards Airforce Base, also testing aircraft off the Navy Carriers. He worked for other contractors testing missiles "ICBMS" for the US Air Force Base. He followed the electronic field into space projects, spy and weather satellites for the US Air Force and Navy. After thirty years of aerospace, he found himself back with the US Navy, testing underseas weapon systems followed by retirement as an author: "A novel thing to do."

CPSIA information can be obtained
at www.ICGtesting.com
Printed in the USA
FFHW021116040919
54765976-60443FF

9 781640 965645